The Trail of the Red Diamonds

A full list of L. Ron Hubbard's
novellas and short stories is provided at the back.

*Dekalogy—a group of ten volumes

L. RON HUBBARD

The Trail of the Red Diamonds

GALAXY
PRESS

Published by
Galaxy Press, LLC
7051 Hollywood Boulevard, Suite 200
Hollywood, CA 90028

Printed in the United States of America.

ISBN-10 1-59212-331-7
ISBN-13 978-1-59212-331-5

Library of Congress Control Number: 2007903544

Contents

Stories from Pulp Fiction's Golden Age

A ND it *was* a golden age.

The 1930s and 1940s were a vibrant, seminal time for a gigantic audience of eager readers, probably the largest per capita audience of readers in American history. The magazine racks were chock-full of publications with ragged trims, garish cover art, cheap brown pulp paper, low cover prices—and the most excitement you could hold in your hands.

"Pulp" magazines, named for their rough-cut, pulpwood paper, were a vehicle for more amazing tales than Scheherazade could have told in a million and one nights. Set apart from higher-class "slick" magazines, printed on fancy glossy paper with quality artwork and superior production values, the pulps were for the "rest of us," adventure story after adventure story for people who liked to *read*. Pulp fiction authors were no-holds-barred entertainers—real storytellers. They were more interested in a thrilling plot twist, a horrific villain or a white-knuckle adventure than they were in lavish prose or convoluted metaphors.

The sheer volume of tales released during this wondrous golden age remains unmatched in any other period of literary history—hundreds of thousands of published stories in over nine hundred different magazines. Some titles lasted only an issue or two; many magazines succumbed to paper shortages during World War II, while others endured for decades yet. Pulp fiction remains as a treasure trove of stories you can read, stories you can love, stories you can remember. The stories were driven by plot and character, with grand heroes, terrible villains, beautiful damsels (often in distress), diabolical plots, amazing places, breathless romances. The readers wanted to be taken beyond the mundane, to live adventures far removed from their ordinary lives—and the pulps rarely failed to deliver.

In that regard, pulp fiction stands in the tradition of all memorable literature. For as history has shown, good stories are much more than fancy prose. William Shakespeare, Charles Dickens, Jules Verne, Alexandre Dumas—many of the greatest literary figures wrote their fiction for the readers, not simply literary colleagues and academic admirers. And writers for pulp magazines were no exception. These publications reached an audience that dwarfed the circulations of today's short story magazines. Issues of the pulps were scooped up and read by over thirty million avid readers each month.

Because pulp fiction writers were often paid no more than a cent a word, they had to become prolific or starve. They also had to write aggressively. As Richard Kyle, publisher and editor of *Argosy*, the first and most long-lived of the pulps, so pointedly explained: "The pulp magazine writers, the best of them, worked for markets that did not write for critics or attempt to satisfy timid advertisers. Not having to answer to anyone other than their readers, they wrote about human beings on the edges of the unknown, in those new lands the future would explore. They wrote for what we would become, not for what we had already been."

Some of the more lasting names that graced the pulps include H. P. Lovecraft, Edgar Rice Burroughs, Robert E. Howard, Max Brand, Louis L'Amour, Elmore Leonard, Dashiell Hammett, Raymond Chandler, Erle Stanley Gardner, John D. MacDonald, Ray Bradbury, Isaac Asimov, Robert Heinlein—and, of course, L. Ron Hubbard.

In a word, he was among the most prolific and popular writers of the era. He was also the most enduring—hence this series—and certainly among the most legendary. It all began only months after he first tried his hand at fiction, with L. Ron Hubbard tales appearing in *Thrilling Adventures, Argosy, Five-Novels Monthly, Detective Fiction Weekly, Top-Notch, Texas Ranger, War Birds, Western Stories,* even *Romantic Range.* He could write on any subject, in any genre, from jungle explorers to deep-sea divers, from G-men and gangsters, cowboys and flying aces to mountain climbers, hard-boiled detectives and spies. But he really began to shine when he turned his talent to science fiction and fantasy of which he authored nearly fifty novels or novelettes to forever change the shape of those genres.

Following in the tradition of such famed authors as Herman Melville, Mark Twain, Jack London and Ernest Hemingway, Ron Hubbard actually lived adventures that his own characters would have admired—as an ethnologist among primitive tribes, as prospector and engineer in hostile climes, as a captain of vessels on four oceans. He even wrote a series of articles for *Argosy*, called "Hell Job," in which he lived and told of the most dangerous professions a man could put his hand to.

Finally, and just for good measure, he was also an accomplished photographer, artist, filmmaker, musician and educator. But he was first and foremost a *writer*, and that's the L. Ron Hubbard we come to know through the pages of this volume.

This library of Stories from the Golden Age presents the best of L. Ron Hubbard's fiction from the heyday of storytelling, the Golden Age of the pulp magazines. In these eighty volumes, readers are treated to a full banquet of 153 stories, a kaleidoscope of tales representing every imaginable genre: science fiction, fantasy, western, mystery, thriller, horror, even romance—action of all kinds and in all places.

Because the pulps themselves were printed on such inexpensive paper with high acid content, issues were not meant to endure. As the years go by, the original issues of every pulp from *Argosy* through *Zeppelin Stories* continue crumbling into brittle, brown dust. This library preserves the L. Ron Hubbard tales from that era, presented with a distinctive look that brings back the nostalgic flavor of those times.

L. Ron Hubbard's Stories from the Golden Age has something for every taste, every reader. These tales will return you to a time when fiction was good clean entertainment and the most fun a kid could have on a rainy afternoon or the best thing an adult could enjoy after a long day at work.

Pick up a volume, and remember what reading is supposed to be all about. Remember curling up with a *great story.*

—Kevin J. Anderson

KEVIN J. ANDERSON *is the author of more than ninety critically acclaimed works of speculative fiction, including The Saga of Seven Suns, the continuation of the Dune Chronicles with Brian Herbert, and his* New York Times *bestselling novelization of L. Ron Hubbard's* Ai! Pedrito!

The Trail of the Red Diamonds

CHAPTER ONE

The Chinese Officer

I first ran across the trail in a hospital, two months after leaving the Gran Chaco behind me. As souvenirs of that continual war I had collected two bullet holes and a case of malaria, and I was certainly in no condition to go racing off to China the way I did.

The doctors told me so and my friends threw up their hands in horror, but that didn't deter me. The urge was too strong. I felt that if I didn't go, I'd be eaten up by the gnawing determination to find the red diamonds of Kublai Khan.

I had come across an original manuscript of Marco Polo's. The man that lent it to me did not know its value. And even when I told him, he laughed at me. I had plenty of money and I didn't need his help, but even so, I had him lined up for a cut in the event of success.

Most copies of Marco Polo's *Travels* leave out a great deal. They have to because it is difficult to decipher, and even more difficult to translate. But, for my own amusement, I had been working on it for almost a month, while laid up.

Halfway through the volume I read a paragraph about a chest of fabulous red stones which glittered "like the sun through red-stained quartz." Stones which would cut even metal. At first I thought he meant rubies. Then, on further description, I understood that he could mean diamonds and only diamonds. Red diamonds.

The things were worth millions! Many millions!

My appetite for the unusual was whetted by that paragraph. I made a note of it for later reference, and it was a good thing that I did. Otherwise I might never have connected it with another, later, item.

Further on in the book, the famous traveler stated that the beliefs of the Asiatics were scarcely understandable to Western minds. He stated further that his host, the emperor of Asia, Kublai Khan, had requested that a chest of glittering red stones be buried with him to light his way to heaven and to serve as offerings to the gods.

Marco Polo, in his painstaking way, had covered years in the writing of his book. The two remarks were far apart in inscription—months, perhaps.

Suddenly I saw the light. I sat up straight in bed, gripping the tattered pages in both hands, shivering with excitement. I was wholly unconscious of my weakened condition, wholly forgetful of the Chaco. I saw only one thing. A chest of red diamonds buried in the grave of Kublai Khan!

I threw the covers back and yelled for my clothes. If Kublai Khan's grave were still intact, it meant that a fortune in rare stones had lain untouched for centuries! And I meant to be the first man there, whether I was sick or well.

An hour later I was in a telegraph station writing a cable to Jim Lange in China. I used a code book that five of us carried. Jim Lange and the other three had been with me in South America, and we had promised when we separated that when anything good turned up, we would let the one nearest to the scene know. As luck would have it, Jim Lange was in Peking.

I had no qualms about setting the whole thing down baldly. No one else would ever know what I wrote. Besides, the code was so condensed that the entire message, including the address, only took eight words.

I told Jim to get a caravan of camels together and to assemble a company of soldiers, and I knew that he would.

Bolstered by excitement, I flew across the continent and sailed from Seattle. Eighteen days later, I was in Kobe, Japan, negotiating a passage on a tub of rust across the Yellow Sea. Five days after that, I was in the Gulf of Campechi, watching the squat concrete forts loom up on the horizon. That evening, I stood outside the railway station at Taku, awaiting the doubtful arrival of a train to Peking, China.

A cold bitter wind was sweeping down from the Gobi, hundreds of miles to the north. Curls of yellow dust swooped around the station's brick corners. Beggars tugged at the skirt of my trench coat, whining for pennies. Soldiers lounged against their baggage, stoically waiting for the train.

I asked the station agent, a wizened Chinese, when the train would come.

"Right away," he said glibly. "Maybe tomorrow morning. Maybe next month. Bandits bad near Tientsin." That was all I could get out of him.

If you've ever been in that hole they call Taku, you'll understand what I was up against. I was racked with excitement. In spite of the wind, I was sweating. And in spite of the sweat, I felt that someone was pouring ice water down my spine. Malaria leaves you that way.

There were no hotels. The station was so filthy that a man couldn't find a place to lie down, but even so, at midnight, I was so tired that I was almost ready to flop in the middle of the platform, coolies and beggars notwithstanding.

It was then that the young Chinese officer in the gray overcoat approached me. It was dark and I couldn't see his face. But by the light from the station window he could see that I was an American.

He asked me if I wanted to go to a hotel. He said that he had just received word from upcountry that the train would not be there until late the next afternoon. He looked at me more closely.

"Whassa matter? You blong sick?"

"I'm all right," I said. "Where's your hotel?"

I let him lead me across the tracks toward a cluster of lights which appeared to be the main part of the ten-house town. When we were a hundred yards away from the station, I could see him only by the green light of a switch.

Then he whirled on me. His stature seemed to double. His hand darted out and caught at my trench coat. I should have been prepared for that, but I was not. Weak and cold and tired, it took me an instant to collect my wits. And that instant was enough for him. His right hand snapped toward my shirt pockets. Something thin and flat and square came away with a rending of cloth.

His left fist smashed me in the mouth, and I staggered back, trying to keep my balance, tripping over the ties. The whole thing took place in a split second. Then he was running, a vague, flitting shadow in the night.

I dropped to my knees and clawed at the side pockets in my artillery boots. Two .25 automatics were there. I jerked both of them out and emptied them as fast as I could pull the triggers.

But I knew I hadn't hit him. I knew he'd gotten away and that there was little use in following. I knew also that I'd meet him some other place.

Crouching in the dark, I felt of my pockets to see what was gone. I searched slowly at first. Then faster. Then frantically. My code book! He had gotten it!

The wind was cold on my teeth. I was swearing in four languages. In a few minutes, I heard running feet and saw the sweep of lanterns coming toward me.

The French colonial troops were swarming down from their barracks, called out by the fourteen shots I had fired. I didn't want to meet the French, and I had been a fool for firing at all.

Another sound clashed with the voices and pounding boots. The train was whistling through the yards down the track on which I stood. I ran toward it. An officer with a flashlight howled at me to stop, but I kept on. The engine clattered past me. Then a car. The train slowed for the station, and I swung aboard.

7

*Two .25 automatics were there. I jerked
both of them out and emptied them as fast
as I could pull the triggers.*

In a compartment I reloaded the guns and shoved them into my boot pockets. I drew up my coat collar and slumped down in the seat. If they saw me through the windows, they didn't come in. They knew that it was useless to search that train, and, besides, the railway is touchy about foreign troops. I sent a porter out after my luggage before we pulled out.

At dawn I was watching my rickshaw boy negotiate the traffic through the great north gate of Peking.

CHAPTER TWO

The Dead Priest

MY space is limited here. I can only cover the high points. Accordingly, then, I must pick up the thread of narrative five days after my arrival in the red-walled, dust-carpeted Peking.

Jim Lange was at the Hotel du Nord. The du Pekin and the Wagon-Lit were preferable, perhaps, but they were too much in evidence. And in the Orient one can never tell who watches.

Jim Lange was about forty, but he looked like a youngster. His hair was gray around his temples, giving the only clue to his age. He was eternally smiling, ever polite, always the Continental gentleman—and he was faster on the draw than any other man I have ever known.

He was upset by the theft of my code book, because it coincided with the theft of my cablegram from his own room. It was evident that someone had guessed our mission and was determined either to stop us or to get there first.

It was quite possible that the man who had looted Jim's room and the one who rifled my pockets were one and the same. I favored that idea. Just how anyone could have gotten wind of the thing was beyond me.

But our expedition was suddenly common knowledge. The fact amazed us not a little, and it amazes me even yet.

11

News travels fast in the Orient. There is something like an underground telegraph which carries its tidings far. Peking, of all the Oriental cities, is probably the worst in that respect.

Five days, then, after my arrival at the du Nord, I was surprised to receive a card from the blue-gowned bellboy. There was nothing on the linen rectangle but a number. That was all. Just "1."

I nodded to bring the caller up. There was nothing else to do. This mysterious number was certainly there on a mission of importance.

In a few seconds, "1" was standing in the hallway, rapping on my door with the handle of his cane. He was a thin, small man with a smooth, unmoving face. He was young, but he looked older than he was. Only his eyes, blue and twinkling, gave him away.

He came in and sat down, but he did not speak until I had poured out a Scotch and soda for him. Holding this before him, he lifted it.

"To your expedition," he said, smiling.

I slapped my glass down on the table and stared at him.

"Don't be alarmed," said "1," sipping his drink. "I'm not after Kublai Khan's grave, and I don't indulge in coffin robbing. If you are surprised that I know of your mission, let it suffice to say that everyone in Peking knows."

If everyone in Peking knew—I should have called the thing off. I should have quit hands down. But I guess I'm too bullheaded for that.

Studying him further, I leaned forward.

"You're British Intelligence. That right?"

"Righto," said "1."

"Then what business of yours is my expedition?"

He laughed, evidently pleased with his role.

"Don't be alarmed, Daly." He pulled a pile of identification papers out of his pocket and spread them out like a hand of cards before my eyes.

"All right," I said. "I guessed it."

"My business with you is prompted by a desire to be of help. And also—well, one must have a little something in return for service."

"You mean," said I, "that you want me to bribe you?"

"I beg your pardon, Daly, but the British Intelligence does not accept bribes."

"Sorry."

"Quite all right, old chap. Quite. The matter I had in mind was of a rather secret nature, but your reputation with the British has always been of the highest."

"Always." I smiled.

"For that reason, I'm giving you help because I want help. Do we understand each other?" When I had nodded, he continued. "We want information from the other side of the Wall. Not very much. Just enough to keep us informed of the movements of the Mikado's troops above Jehol. It is a rather simple task, but, unfortunately, the last three men we sent up there have failed to return.

"You are a good blind, that's all," continued "1." "I would like to send an intelligence officer with you. He will guide you across the country, and he will help you if you should happen to cross the paths of any warlords up there. He would have complete authority to grant you anything the British have to offer. He would do his own work on the side, and you need never bother with it."

"All right," I said. "Send him over to the hotel tonight with credentials. We are leaving rather early in the morning. All our camels are in line and we have about thirty fighting men who are to meet us outside the city. It's agreed."

He left, then, and it was the last I ever saw of him.

At three o'clock, Jim came in and I told him what had happened. But he didn't seem to be listening to me. His blue eyes were restless, and he kept staring out into the alley below our window as though he wished I'd hurry up and finish what I had to say so that he could get his word in.

"I was up to the Hall of Classics this afternoon," Jim merely said, when I had finished.

Something in the way he said it told me that he had found a clue. The Hall of Classics is not a hall at all, but a large courtyard filled with obelisks or something of that sort on which the sayings of Confucius have been written.

"I found an old Chinaman," continued Jim. "He was in there studying to get a higher clerk rating."

Jim always liked to do the dramatic thing and so he left his remarks hanging in midair while he poured and downed a drink to wash the Peking dust out of his throat.

"This old Chinaman was wise," continued Jim. "And for

no reason at all, he turned around to me and told me that the chart I sought would be found in the Lama temple."

"It's a trap," I stated.

"No. I don't know why, but it isn't. This whole town knows what we're up to and the old fellow was just fishing for a good-sized tip, which I gave him."

"You're crazy," I snapped. "That's the only sure way they could get us!"

"Keep calm," replied Jim, unruffled. "I've been in the country longer than you have and I speak the lingo. I know a straight Chinese when I see him, and this old boy was one. He was a clerk and they can't afford to lie. One fib and their heads go off."

"One slip and our heads disappear, too," I said.

"Admitted," agreed Jim Lange. "But it's worth the chance. After all, our leads are pretty sparse."

"They are that. All right, as long as you say so, I'll go over to the Lama temple with you and—say! The Lama temple is closed and has been closed for the last three years. Am I right?"

He nodded, knowingly. "That's the point. We'll have to scale the wall and get in somehow. But if I were you, I'd stay here. It's liable to be—"

"Forget it! I'm as well as you are." Which, of course, was a lie.

At five o'clock we left the hotel and took rickshaws down toward the Forbidden City and Coal Hill. Under any other conditions, I would have drawn the line. But the red diamonds were blazing magnets which drew us into incredible complications. They robbed us of our caution and stilled whatever misgivings we might have felt. We were ready to do anything to gain the possession of those stones.

Anything!

The Lama temple was gray and foreboding through the dusk. The grimy walls were frowning and rough and the gates were barred shut, nailed by the order of authorities. Too much evil and unrest had exuded from this place before it had been closed. Too many mysteries had surrounded it. And it was whispered that strange rites were still conducted behind those bars—that there were secret tunnels underneath the walls, entered from the grave mounds on Coal Hill.

We stopped before the gates. Vendors tried to catch our eyes, but they would not come close to us—would not approach those high, dull gates before which we stood. I thought I caught a furtive movement in the shadows across the street, but I was not sure. Besides, my nerves were jumpy.

If this were a trap, we would have to fight out of it with lead. And in that case Peking would be too hot for us. But I was amazed at the certainty of knowledge which was suddenly seeping through me. I seemed to know that this was the place our quest should start.

And then Jim was pulling at my sleeve and we were hidden in a jog of the wall, pressing back against the gray stone, waiting. No one came after us. The sounds on the street were the same. Assured, I dug my fingers into the crevices of the wall and started up. Jim helped me by shoving on my boot soles.

At the top, I did not linger. A man makes a plain silhouette even against a black sky. I threw myself over like a pole vaulter.

I seemed to fall for a hundred feet. But when my boots jarred against the stone, I knew it had been fifteen at the most. Jim thudded down beside me and we stood there in the blackness, peering through the darkness of the courtyard.

The silence was tense. This place, supposed to be deserted, was filled with moving shadows. Perhaps they were caused by the waving of trees in the wind, but however that might be, my heart was pounding with a dull, throbbing beat. Death waited there across the yard. I could feel it.

We walked forward on cat feet, watching every movement. My boots sounded like cannon shots across the stone. Ahead of us something which was neither wind nor shadow moved.

I sprinted ahead. The movement was quick. Soft footfalls hurried away. I dived off in pursuit. Jim was behind me, starting off in another direction, but I was so intent on my quarry that I did not notice. If this were a Lama priest, then, perhaps, I could persuade him to divulge the information I craved. If it were another—perhaps the soldier of Taku—then I had a score to settle. The big butt of a .45 was solid against my palm.

Jim was lost in the maze of buildings. My lungs felt like hot coals in my chest. The man I followed suddenly turned and stood calmly waiting for me. I could not see his face, nor more than the outline of his body, but I sensed a smile on his lips.

I slacked my pace, juggled the gun and came nearer.

"Whassa matter?" squeaked my quarry. "You allasamee loco, huh?"

I stopped. The muzzle of my gun traveled down. I felt that

this must be a priest. Then suddenly I remembered the voice. It was that of the soldier of Taku!

I jumped aside. But he did not shoot. Instead, he whirled and ran toward a blank wall.

"Stop!" I shouted.

But he kept on. I threw the gun up waist high and sent a snapped shot after him. The report rolled through the courtyard like mighty thunder.

The flash of powder had blinded me for an instant. When I could see again, I sprinted forward.

Where the blank wall had been, there was a ray of light. Then it was gone! The courtyard, bound in by solid stone, was empty save for myself!

I gasped. Approaching the wall, I felt of the rock. There were no holes which might betray a hidden door. Nothing but blank stone. My soldier friend had been swallowed up!

Then I heard Jim yelling for me and I went back. It was a long way, and I was surprised that I had run so far. But I found Jim.

He was standing over a bundle of something, looking down at it.

"We were a little too late," he said, simply.

I looked at the bundle. It was a man—a dead man. A Lama priest whose robes were drenched with warm blood and whose hands were stretched out in front of him, clutching at unyielding stone. From his back protruded the handle of a knife—a bayonet.

"Too late," Jim repeated. "If we had been here a little sooner, we might have—"

"Wait," I said. "This was a trap. But they expected that only you would come. Two was one too many for them. They thought to put you out of the way so that they could deal with me alone—and they know that I'm not in exactly top-notch physical condition. That man I chased was waiting for you."

Jim nodded and then kneeled down beside the corpse. Gingerly he rolled the thing over on its back. The greasy yellow robes were wet and sticky. I saw something shiny in the priest's left hand. In an instant I had recovered it.

"A Buddha," I said. "He died with his idol."

Jim nodded again and took the thing from me. It was small, exquisitely carved, from ivory stained brown by countless ages. Jim handed it back. But I was shaking with exhaustion and excitement. I dropped it to the stone.

There was a dull pop. I stared down at it. "Why . . . why, my God, Jim, the thing's hollow!"

He scooped it up once more and felt of the base. He shoved his fingernails into every conceivable crevice, into the creases which outlined the fingers and the toes, into the eyes and nose and mouth. But the image was still smiling, still fat, still intact. In his anxiety, Jim crushed it between his thumb and index finger.

Abruptly, the bottom dropped out of it and—across the flagged yard rolled a thing which was as bright as blood, as brilliant as flame. A red diamond!

19

CHAPTER THREE

The Death of a Spy

AT the hotel we went immediately to our room. The Buddha in my pocket felt as though it weighed a thousand pounds—every pound white hot. When I entered the room I was so busy with my own speculations that it took me two or three seconds to realize that another man was there.

He was thin, short, pink-cheeked. He was young, and from his clothes and expression one would have judged him to be a casual tourist. I had scarcely taken in his build and expression when I saw something else. A thin line of red across the side of his throat.

He got up off the bed and set down his glass.

"Oh, hullo there. You're Daly, aren't you?"

"Yes," I nodded. "And you're—?"

"The man '1' sent." He reached into his coat pocket and brought out a packet of papers from which he extracted a note.

"This," said the note, "is Greg McDonald. He will help you." It was signed with the numeral one.

I shoved out my hand and he took it. His eyes were level and coolly appraising, for all his young smile. I glanced over his other papers and then introduced him to Jim.

It was Jim who noticed the blood on the floor.

"Where the devil did that come from?" he demanded.

21

The visitor glanced at it and shrugged. Then he pointed at my hands which were stained red. He grinned.

"I might do well to ask you chaps about it also."

"A dead priest," I said.

"A dead spy," replied Greg McDonald. He went over to the window, threw it wide open and stepped back, pointing down at the cobblestoned alley.

We were only about five feet from the ground and I swung through and dropped beside the huddled form. The man had landed on his face and the sight was not pleasant. The skin was yellow, the eyes black. The man wore a gray overcoat and carried a small saber. I had a feeling that it was my soldier from Taku.

Greg McDonald, leaning from the window, shrugged again when I looked up.

"He was here, hiding when I came," he explained. "He tackled me and scratched me with his nails. Sorry, but I had to kill him, and after he fell out the window, I was darned if I'd lift him back through again. You know how it is."

I climbed back.

"This means we'll have to get out of the city tonight. If we wait until tomorrow, the authorities will get on to it."

"Oh," said McDonald, "you needn't hurry. I'm sure I can straighten it out with the powers that be."

"No," I demurred, "we can't risk that. We've found the clue we wanted." I took the Buddha out of my pocket and threw it on the bed. Then I pulled the red diamond out of my pocket and let it blaze in the light.

"My heavens!" cried McDonald, jostled out of his British calm. "You . . . you . . . where did you get that?"

"That would be telling," said Jim, softly.

"But—" stammered McDonald, "I—I never saw anything so beautiful as that thing. You mean to tell me you know where there are others?"

"Perhaps," said Jim. "And I agree with John. We've got to get out of here tonight. There's no time for delay. Somebody else is on this trail. They killed the priest and searched him. And they missed the Buddha in their rush. We found it. And—" He stopped, staring at the back of the small, grinning idol.

Jim scooped it up, devouring it with his eyes. Then he sighed and looked up at the ceiling as though he prayed.

"Not only a red diamond," he murmured. "Not only a red diamond, but also a chart." He passed it to me. "See that series of lines on the back? That one is the Great Wall. You can guess at the others."

I forgot about McDonald. I forgot about the dead man outside the window. I forgot everything except the grave of Kublai Khan. Except the chest of stones which would have lit the emperor's path to heaven.

The red diamonds were waiting for us, up across the Wall, across the plains, through the lines of warring armies, across mountains. In my palm, the Buddha smiled.

23

CHAPTER FOUR

The Stolen Buddha

OUR camels were waiting for us outside the Hataman Gate. The north gate was, of course, the obvious point of departure, but I felt that we would stand a better chance of getting away unobserved if we used the Hataman, which was but three or four blocks from the du Nord Hotel.

The number of our beasts was great. Twenty of them. But the very number excused us from secrecy. Ostensibly we were a trading expedition moving north toward the Gobi.

My horse was a Mongolian pony, and I think the breed deserves some slight mention. His nose was a sledgehammer and his eyes, small and evil, were hidden under a gigantic cowlick. His entire body was covered with long hair. He came almost to my shoulder, but my weight was nothing to him.

A month before he had been utterly untamed, but now he was fairly docile. He would only bite when your back was turned.

The saddle was of Cossack design. Two crosstrees in tandem with a leather pillow buckled down between them. The strap across the pillow is the secret of a Cossack's ability to ride standing up. He hooks his toes through the belt and the possibility of falling off is slight.

We swung out toward Nankou, a long line of grunting, grumbling beasts and sleepy men. The soldiers fell in on either side of us, carrying their guns in every conceivable position. They were late of several bandit armies and their weapons were everything from Mannlichers to Springfields. We had nothing heavier or faster than a rifle, but with thirty-two men, we felt fairly safe from attack.

That was a mistake. A man who sells his services to the highest bidder feels no qualms about changing flags on short notice—especially when the side he first chose is losing.

Everything went smoothly for the first three days. We crossed the Wall through Nankou Pass and struck out ahead. But on the evening of the fourth day, just after we had made camp in a slight depression of ground, I scented trouble.

Two sentries stood just on the rim of camp. They were talking in a loud singsong and they held their rifles at port. I watched them. They seemed to become more angry with each passing moment. Suddenly one of them struck out with a rifle butt and felled the other. The victim bounced to his feet, bayonet shimmering wickedly.

I jumped up and started to run toward them. A hand restrained me. It was Jim Lange. I stopped and turned angrily, trying to shake him off.

"Don't approach them," said Jim. "That's an old ruse. They want to get you near them and then, while you're separating them, they'll turn on you and pick your pockets."

A moment later they stood back from each other and shot nervous glances in my direction. They looked sheepish. Presently they resumed their posts without a word.

That night I performed an operation in my tent. I took an indelible pencil and traced the map of the Buddha on my thigh. Then I took a jackknife and scratched the marks until they bled. It hurt like the very devil, but I knew that it was necessary. I knew also that I risked infection.

After I had finished I took a ten percent solution of iodine and smeared the square. It completely hid the lines. I knew that a little alcohol would remove the iodine so that I could read the map. It was the only thing I could do.

After that I scraped the original off the Buddha, put it back in the accustomed pocket and went to sleep. During the night I thought I heard a furtive movement in my tent, but I paid it little heed. I would have been wide awake had anyone come within three feet of my cot.

In the morning, the Buddha was gone!

But I had the map. I still have it and I will always have it, until they blow taps over my six square feet of real estate. But the map is only in symbols. I alone know the meaning of the lines, know which is north, know just what the scale is. Twice, since I left China, I have been attacked. But I do not think it will happen again. It takes more than fire to bring out the scale, the orientation and the proper lettering.

I didn't tell Jim and McDonald about it. They had enough to worry about. But I did tell them to watch the two sentries. For three days, nothing else happened. And then we reached the pass in the mountains.

27

CHAPTER FIVE

Precipice of Death

O N referring to my somewhat bedraggled diary, I find that we sighted the pass at about four in the afternoon. McDonald identified it for us. He seemed to know his way through this country. He told me that it had an L twist in the middle and that tallied with my chart.

He also told me that he thought it would be better if he took a side trip that he had in mind. He didn't say what he wanted to do. Some Japanese soldiers were quartered about fifteen miles away and I expected that McDonald would gather some information there. He was very nervous as he dressed, and I didn't blame him. It isn't the pleasantest thing in the world to have to walk into a Japanese encampment after dark.

He put on a brown dye and a wiry-haired wig and donned a red-tabbed, mustard-colored uniform. Then he turned his saddle blanket over and I saw that the insignia of a Japanese regiment was embroidered on the reverse side.

He wanted to know where he could pick us up if he lived to tell the tale and I informed him that we would probably push right on through that night.

Young McDonald was plainly aghast.

"But, Daly! I say, old chap, but you know something might happen in there. It's bad, very bad. Some of the trail goes along the side of a precipice and the drop is better than a thousand feet in one place. You might lose several of your camels. I strictly would not advise it."

I shook my head. "If anyone wants to ambush us, this is the place for it. They'd have to make an open order charge on the plain. This is the last pass we go through. And I don't want the sun up there showing us up as targets. Get it?"

"You mean you'd rather be attacked in the dark?" gasped McDonald.

"Why not? Only sound will tell them that we're coming and the precipice won't make any difference. They'll think twice—whoever they are—before they go rough-and-tumble along a five-foot ledge. It will all be volley fire and that isn't so effective."

"Why, you speak as though you really thought you would be ambushed," said McDonald.

"I think we will be. Some of these soldiers aren't shooting square with us." I jerked my thumb at a grizzled Tartar sergeant. "Among others, I think he's against us. That would be very bad—a mutiny in the pass. But at night—well, you see, they'll think of their own hides, too.

"And another thing. Men have been hanging around our fires who do not belong to us. They thought I did not see them, but I did."

Greg McDonald sighed, threw a foot into his stirrup and went up. The Mongol pony snorted and sidestepped quickly. McDonald, a perfect Japanese officer, raised his hand to us in salute, drove home the spurs and became a dwindling swirl of dust across the plain.

We camped there, resting and waiting for the moonlight I knew would come. We made camels' dung fires and boiled water for tea. The Mongolians in the party added butter to their steaming cups. I tried it and found it good.

The moon came up, twice as big as it should have been. At first it looked like a fire over the horizon's rim and then it was with us, making the plain fill itself with shadows. The pass looked like a gun sight ahead of us. At the first glimmer we started to move off.

When we had gained the entrance of the pass, I went ahead on the scout. McDonald had not told me wrong. Less than a thousand yards from the mouth, the bed of a river started to drop away like a falling bomb. At half a mile, the cut was merely a deep black hole. The path went up because our way and the river's course parted at the L.

We started moving the camels through, and their grunted protests must have reached far. The ponies' hoofs struck fire from the flinty debris which cluttered the trail. Above us the moon filled half the gorge with light. We were in the lighted half.

A quarter of a mile before we got to the L, Jim worked his way up beside me.

"I don't like this a bit," he said. "They can sit over there and snipe us off. I wish we'd thought about it before."

"Too late now. Whoever it is that's messing into our business would hardly pass up such a chance as this. Even if he's just one man, he wouldn't find it hard to muster a company of loose soldiers. They'd do it for the loot alone."

I spurred ahead of the caravan. Jim dropped far behind it, urging the stragglers. That move saved our lives.

The first bullet came just as I rounded the L. It smacked stone above my head and went whining on down the trail into the thick of the camels. Instead of drawing up, I dug in my rowels. The pony leaped ahead. At my right I could see the dark abyss. I did not know what lay ahead.

I did not know the exact plan, but before long I understood. In fact, within the next ten seconds.

Stone grumbled high up on our wall. A vague, sighing sound, doubling, tripling into crescendo until it threatened to blast me out of my already precarious saddle.

They had started an avalanche above us. Tons of rock crashed and roared down the hillside. Camels bawled. Men screamed. Bedlam broke loose behind me. I drew in and flung myself down behind my horse. There was nothing I could do. I did not know whether or not Jim was still alive and the anxiety of it made me a little sick. But I gripped the .45 and watched for another rifle flame.

Looking back, I saw a camel teetering near the edge. A soldier had hold of his halter, tugging at it. The shower of rocks thickened. For an instant I could see nothing for dust. Then I saw the camel start to fall. His hindquarters went first. He scrambled to regain his footing. The soldier fought to free himself of the rein. The camel rocked back. Darkness and the sound of hammering rocks swallowed them and their screams.

A gun flared yellow-white ahead. I shot straight into the

blaze. A man pitched out from the cover and fell, turning over and over through a thousand feet. A .45 slug takes them that way.

The avalanche quieted to a fitful rumble. The moon was higher now and I could see that the trail, wonder of wonders, was still intact. Most of the debris had bounced off an overhang, but not high enough to miss men and camels.

I did not care so badly about the camels. They were becoming excess baggage. They had served their purpose as a blind. And after the traitorous tricks the men had pulled, I could not feel too badly about them. But where was Jim?

At last I saw him. Running low, leading his terrified pony, he sprinted across the cleared zone and came up to me.

"They're all gone!" he cried.

I knew it before he told me, but the utterance of the knowledge gave me a far worse shock than the witnessing of it had.

"Get on and ride!" I yelled. "They're all around us!"

We could have been clearly seen in the moonlight. But we were going fast along that precarious ledge and we were a difficult target to hit. The thunder of hoofs drowned the sounds of shots behind us. Once I caught the splinter of a bullet against rock above me. They were shooting at us then.

Someone stood on the trail before us. Without checking our pace, I yanked out the .45 and held it ready. I saw a rifle whip up to the level of my eyes. I fired between my pony's ears. A shadow tumbled through space, glittering when the moon struck the rifle.

I fired between my pony's ears. A shadow tumbled through space, glittering when the moon struck the rifle.

Headlong down the trail we plunged, with death whispering in our ears and with death tugging at us from below. The trail leveled out under us and led away to a plateau. We were far out on the plain before we stopped. I sat with my head on my chest, breathing harder than my horse.

Jim came up and threw himself off his mount.

"Pretty tough," he said. I nodded. "Do you suppose they'll hit us again?" he asked.

I knew he merely wanted to be reassured. But I felt all gone inside.

"Sure they will. They did that just to get rid of our equipment and our armed forces. Now, they'll be able to take us without much of a fight. All we can do is to push on hard and get there before they do."

"But what about McDonald?"

"I guess he'll get along. We can't do anything for him now. Let's ride."

Jim mounted and we rode.

When dawn came we were near our destination, and when the light was good enough I took a pair of field glasses and went to a high point of land to study the plateau we had just quitted.

Everything was yellow. The mountains were craggy and harsh even in the distance, and the wind moaned through the cleft in which I lay. Never before have I seen such desolate, utterly wasted country.

Far to the east I could see a horseman coming. Behind him, about two miles, I could see a swirl of dust which soon became a racing cavalry troop. But the troop could not see their quarry as I could.

I studied the man in the lead. At last I made out a set of red tabs and a yellow face. I knew then that it was McDonald. His eyes were set and his mouth was tight. He was riding for his life, from the looks of things.

In a few minutes he swung down into a gulch and ran along the hard rock bottom, losing his trail. When the cavalry came to the place, they galloped onward in a straight line.

Going down, I told Jim to saddle up once more. I buckled my own cinch and we rode out to the end of the gully and found McDonald. He looked about done in.

"They found out who I was," he wheezed, tiredly. "You can't fool those little devils. They were going to skin me alive, but I got away."

Somehow, that remark about skinning him alive grated on me. I carried a tattooed chart on my leg, and for the first time it occurred to me that to get that chart, a man would have to rip off my hide.

CHAPTER SIX

The Human Sacrifice

I'M sorry I cannot set down the exact formation of the land about the burial temple of Kublai Khan. If I did that, I am afraid that a topographical study of the ground would reveal the exact location. But I can tell you how it looked.

We found it with ridiculous ease, setting at the far end of a big gully. Why Kublai Khan had wanted to be buried in such a place, I did not know. I was not well enough acquainted with his history. But I believe that, in that day, the bodies of rulers were extremely valuable. So much so, in fact, that armies invaded territories to exhume and steal the coffins of kings. For one king to possess the body of another was much like possessing his scepter.

Accordingly, Kublai Khan had so decreed, I suppose, that his grave would never be molested. He had caused himself to be buried in the most hidden part of his kingdom. And a man as great as Kublai Khan could be sure that his wishes would be carried out even after death.

I had expected a pagoda of some sort, but instead we found that the hut had a flat roof. It was all of stone, and the men who built it had been certain that their work would endure for centuries.

But they did not build the entire tomb above the ground.

Most of it lies far below. I doubt if it would even be noticed from an airplane, for it is the color of the terrain—yellow.

I'm afraid that the sight of the place made me a little crazy. I jumped off my horse and raced pell-mell for the low, open door, pulling at the flashlight which hung from my belt. Jim called to me to wait, but I dashed on ahead, completely disregarding him. The thought of red diamonds—a chest of red diamonds—was too much for me.

Ahead of me there might lie an ambush. Ahead there might be age-old traps. I'm not especially a daredevil, but I didn't seem to care. I plunged through the opening and shot on my light.

I had expected to see a room, perhaps a crypt, but all I saw was a black tunnel stretching into the bowels of the earth. My feet carried me down, but I felt as though I floated in midair.

The place was odorous with age and as I went down the passage I could hear the ceaseless drip of water ahead of me. The walls became damp, covered with a green slime. I traveled far. There were two tunnels there, and at the fork I hesitated long enough to realize that Jim had not followed me. But I supposed that he would be along as soon as he had hidden the horses.

Taking the right branch, I found that I was once more going down. Steps had been cut into the stone and the descent was easy, though steep. Abruptly I found myself on the threshold of a large room.

My flashlight played over the walls and then came to rest on the portion farthest away from me. Chills raced up and down my back as I saw that sight. The thing was too utterly real, too terrible, too gruesome.

It was an idol, a war god, squatting on massive stone haunches, watching me out of glittering red eyes. He looked as though he were about to speak. His jaw was loose, as though it could be moved. Before him lay a platform of stone, with grooves running diagonally down its sides.

I knew what that was. I had seen blocks like that in the Maya country, in Angkor Wat, in the South Pacific. It was a sacrificial altar and the grooves were made for the hot, running blood of human victims.

At last I tore my eyes away from the war god. A passage lay to the idol's left and I took it, continuing to travel down. How far this lies below the surface, I have no way of knowing. It would require a better civil engineer than I am to determine its twisting depth.

The darkness seemed to thicken. Silence reigned. The clanking of my boot heels on stone seemed a desecration of the tomb. Then another, larger room opened before me. Its ceiling was high, almost beyond the range of my flashlight. The floor was level and moss-grown.

In the center of the stones sat a rectangle of stone. I knew then that I had found the tomb of Kublai Khan, lost to the world for centuries!

Perhaps the crypt had at one time been decorated with crossed swords, a shield, spears. But these were only piles of black rust now. Nothing was left but the imperishable stone.

With trembling hands I tore at the head blocks. They came away with surprising ease. I threw them aside. I dislodged the slabs, unconscious that I ripped the nails from my fingers. But I did not have far to go.

A coffin had lain there at one time, but it was gone. The body of a mighty emperor had been there, but dust had claimed it back. Save for a few bands of copper and a golden ring, the vault was empty!

At first I thought that the red diamonds might lie beneath the crypt, but the floor was obviously undisturbed. It was solid rock. I searched along the walls, looking for a niche, but there was none.

I stopped in the center of the room, staring at the vault, completely baffled. This, certainly, was going to be more than a one-man job. I thought that I had better find McDonald and Jim. Suiting action to thought, I sprinted up the ramp toward the room of the war god.

It is difficult to write about what I found there. Even the thought of it still makes me feel sick and weary. I remember that I stood for some minutes, unable to take my eyes from the gruesome spectacle.

Jim Lange lay there. On the sacrificial altar. His throat had been cut, his shirt was tattered and soggy where the killer had plunged a savage knife innumerable times. The blood ran down the grooves to the floor and collected there in black puddles.

I had no idea how it had happened. Perhaps the Japanese had been there, waiting for us. Perhaps the tomb had guards, after all these centuries. Perhaps—well, there was no use speculating about it. Jim Lange was dead on a sacrificial block and all the deduction in the world could not bring him back to life.

I guess I went a little crazy then. I don't know what I said. I only know that I dragged Jim's body from that terrible bed and that I found the red diamonds!

They were concealed in the altar. Any slight movement of the top caused the entire surface to raise up as though on springs. My flashlight hammered into a cauldron of red, glowing diamonds.

I laid Jim Lange on the floor and crossed his arms over his chest. Then I went back to the altar and ran my hands through the glittering wealth. I was stunned, out on my feet. But the diamonds did not seem to represent money or any of the things that a man can buy. They had meant the death of Jim Lange.

I scooped up a double handful and threw them from me. They scattered out like seeds, rolling drops of red along the floor. Some of them were sticky where the blood had leaked through the cracks.

Everything must have gone blank at that point, for I remember nothing more until I got outside. McDonald was standing by the horses.

CHAPTER SEVEN

Before the War God

B RACING myself against the stone doorway, I stared at him. The sight of his familiar face jerked me out of a period a thousand years old and brought me back to the twentieth century. He steadied me. "What's happened?" he asked.

"Jim is dead," I said as calmly as possible.

"Dead? But . . . but how can he be dead? He left me just a moment ago."

"He's dead, all right," I repeated, dully. "And I found the diamonds. Do you want to see them?"

His eyes lit up. He walked quickly toward me, past me and down the tunnel. I pointed the way for him with my flashlight and walked slowly after him. He took the right-hand bend and then stopped. I threw my flash on the war god and he gasped.

"They're over there in the altar," I said almost without interest. "They must have been set there as a sacrifice to their god."

McDonald did not seem to notice Jim. Somehow, the lack of interest in the body of my friend enraged me. It was like a blow, somehow. I might have argued that McDonald was used to such things, but I was almost past the point of reason.

43

McDonald knelt quickly beside the altar and ran his fingers through the glittering mass. He seemed to be talking to himself—or perhaps talking to the diamonds. He looked up at me—and in that instant I was jerked out of my lethargy by the sudden knowledge that McDonald was utterly mad!

"They're mine," he drooled. His face was no longer boyish. It was hard and old and vicious.

"Snap out of it!" I shouted. "We're two white men alone in this confounded country. We'll never get out alive unless we stick together! For God's sake, man, don't look at me that way!"

"They're mine," he said and then he repeated it over and over with the monotonous intonation of a chant. Behind him the war god's red eyes were glowing coals. There was a similarity between the two. The droop of the mouth—McDonald turned his back on me and stared into the mass of brilliance.

And then the war god spoke! The jaw moved and the eyes seemed to increase their fire.

"They're his! Go before you die!"

I stepped backward. I could feel the hair rise on the back of my neck. I was stripped of every civilized vestige in that instant. I was a savage standing before a powerful, ancient god. And the god's word was law!

But the trick was not destined to work. My flashlight sagged and, in sagging, caught and held a blue glimmer of steel in McDonald's hand. I shot my fingers to the automatics in my boot tops, but I was not quick enough. Flame lanced out from McDonald's waistline. The slug caught me in the

44

left side, just under the heart. But I was conscious of no pain. Only a terrifying numbness.

My fingers found the automatics' butts. I straightened. The flashlight rolled along the floor, forgotten, but it did its work well. It rested the icy beam square on McDonald's twisted face, blinding him.

I did not know that he was blinded, then, though I know it now. I only knew that I had found the killer. Firing with a slow, deliberate speed, I blotted out his face. Left gun, right gun, left gun, right gun. I suppose it would be called murder, but he was the man who had killed Jim.

McDonald sagged, dead at the first shot. Limply he sprawled across the grooves, pouring his own life's stream into them. Above him the war god's eyes were thin and brittle. Left gun, right gun. The dead body leaped and quivered under the impact of slugs.

Then my magazines were empty and the click of the empty chambers was my signal to crumple. But even after I fell flat on my face, I managed to inch forward to make sure that McDonald was dead. I can remember how his face looked to this day.

After that everything was blurred. I must have bandaged the hole in my side, though I do not remember doing so. I must have dragged myself out to a pony and somehow I must have mounted. Later I found three diamonds in my pockets. That surprises me, because I could hardly have realized that I would need their wealth back in civilization.

One scene will always be with me. I wake at night to find

that it hovers above my face. The scene of that room, drowned in powder smoke, with the war god's red eyes glaring through the curling haze!

What I knew instinctively then, I know for certain now. McDonald was Jim's murderer.

McDonald was not McDonald at all, but some renegade. In some way he had caught word of Jim's activities in hiring troops and buying camels. He had evidently followed Jim back to his hotel and had then rifled the room, finding and taking the code message.

Knowing that he had to have a key, he found out who I was—probably in Jim's correspondence—and then came down to Taku to wait for my arrival. When I came, he had no great difficulty in picking me out. Americans are few at that port and one can spot a tourist.

This renegade had disguised himself as a Chinese officer. He had attacked me solely for the purpose of getting the code key which he knew I must carry. Why he did not take Jim's I don't know. Maybe Jim kept his in a safer place than I did.

But my main reason for knowing it was "McDonald," came from the fact that the Chinese officer struck me with a fist. Chinese never use their fists.

"McDonald" was also the old Chinaman at the Hall of Classics. He wanted Jim to go to the Lama temple because he thought that Jim would go alone and that he could be killed there. Evidently, "McDonald" had but very little money. He had obviously contracted with the Lama priest to obtain the Buddha.

Unable to pay for it in cash, "McDonald" killed the priest and then tried to find the Buddha. But the statue in the priest's hand was not easily seen and we had come upon "McDonald" as he started to look for it. He made his getaway through a passage which I could not find.

When we got back to the hotel, "McDonald" was waiting for us. He had found the real British agent there, had killed him, and had thrown the body out of the window, after dressing it in the Chinese uniform and coloring the face. Of course, the renegade had taken the officer's papers. The scar on "McDonald's" throat had been made by my bullet earlier in the evening.

Then, "McDonald" left us just before the attack. Wanting us to believe that he was a real agent, he dressed himself as a Japanese officer. He had stolen the Buddha, discovered that the map had been erased from it. He knew, therefore, that he had to kill us to get it, and he did not want to fight fairly. Hence, the ambush by which he rid himself of his agents among our men that he could no longer use.

But, unfortunately for "McDonald," he had run across a patrol of Japanese cavalry and had had to ride for his life.

He had killed Jim while I was below ground, and he had intended to kill me just as soon as he was led to the red diamonds. He tried to scare me out by making the idol talk—a ventriloquist's trick—but, failing that, he had had to shoot me.

Well, no matter now. My only regret is for the real McDonald. We left him, unknowing, cursing him, stabbed to death in a filthy alley of Peking.

I arrived at a port of the Yellow Sea with the aid of two peasants. I don't know how they kept me alive during the trip, but they did, and I paid them well for it. I stayed there in a hospital, recuperating.

At first the British were hostile. They tried to hang the murder of the real McDonald upon me, and I could not send them to the temple of Kublai Khan. I wanted to go back there myself. They compromised by sending me out of the country.

It's all patched up now, and I can go back. Perhaps "1" had something to do with it.

Most of the money I received for the three red diamonds has been spent now. I shall go back this year, winter though it is. But this time I am not trusting Chinese soldiers. I have already recruited a company of fighting Americans!

Hurricane's Roar

Chapter One

H O, ho," cried Tsing the Fool, "it is long since I have laughed. When the gods deliver Wind-Gone-Mad into our hands, we will again taste the sweet fruits of fortune—and perhaps other sweeter pleasures. The rewards say he is better delivered dead."

Thus he spoke to his nodding aide before the red wall of the ruined temple. About the two stood soldiers in gray cotton uniforms, padded against the past winter's chill. The soldiers were not smiling. They stood uneasily in the yellow dust, shifting their rifles from hand to hand, glancing nervously at the saffron sky.

The big square poster bore the Mongol scrawl in bold, vertical columns. Freely translated, it said:

> At high noon tomorrow, I will appear over your camp. Spread a white cloth before your headquarters as a sign that you agree to my terms. If the ground is blank, then I come to attack, to destroy and to kill.
>
> Your war is foolish and it does not fit with my requirements. It must be stopped. Otherwise I am the judge, my gavel is my machine gun, my sentence is death.
>
> Wind-Gone-Mad

"Excellency," said a tight-faced captain, "perhaps it would be better to appear to agree with this one. The sun is riding higher."

Tsing the Fool whirled upon the captain. Tsing the Fool was dressed in a blue silk jacket, a pair of highly polished boots and a round cap which sat squarely over his plump and jovial face. Tsing the Fool was filled with laughter and when he laughed his body shook like clabbered milk. Only his ink-dot eyes were cruel.

"Run from one man?" wheezed Tsing the Fool. "I strike colors to none!"

"But this fellow," said the captain hesitantly, "is known to be . . . thorough in everything he undertakes. Wind-Gone-Mad will not like it if you choose to argue with him."

"Bah, he is a myth conjured up by cowards. What one man could do all the things he is supposed to have done? He will not dare attack us. One man against my forces? Ho, ho!"

"Nevertheless, I have seen him in action. I was at Shiu when he downed two bombers in the breath of a gnat."

Tsing the Fool turned to his aide. "Place machine guns all about this square. Mount a pair of small-bore cannon in the open. Pack the roof of the monastery with riflemen. We will bring him down if he comes. No one is to fire until I blow the signal. And, Chu, spread me that white sheet in case he forgets to come within range."

A murmur of awe ran through the crowd. Silence fell upon them. They all heard the drumming snarl of a mighty engine far out in the sky. They all knew that Wind-Gone-Mad was coming. Knuckles whitened, bolts snicked, the aide was spreading the table cloth.

Two days before, in the Hotel du Pekin, a casual meeting had started Wind-Gone-Mad upon his way. Two days before a man named Lawrence Martin had knocked upon the door of Jim Dahlgren.

Martin was a man of about forty, a man with visionary eyes and the quiet air of an empire builder.

Jim Dahlgren was lean-limbed, alert, dressed neatly as became a salesman for Amalgamated Aeronautical Company. Martin accepted a chair and came straight to the point.

"I am here in the interest of the Panama-Pacific Airlines, Dahlgren."

Jim Dahlgren had smiled with half his mouth, a quizzical smile, with something reckless in it. "Peking, China is a long ways from Panama, Martin. I don't get your drift."

"Not so far either, young fellow. You might have heard that we completed our survey trip across the Pacific. We are ready to start regular service to Shanghai from San Francisco. And more than that, we are ready to survey an express route from Shanghai to Peking, from Peking to Moscow and thence to Europe."

"That's a long route. Having any trouble?"

"Plenty of it."

"But why look for me?"

"Because you are supposed to know this country backwards and you're supposed to have an eye on Mongolia. I want you to act as intermediary for us in a matter up north."

"Glad to. What is it?"

"I understand that there are two armies fighting in central Inner Mongolia. This obstructs our route. We must have a field midway between here and Urga. The scene of that war is also, unhappily, the only logical place we can choose. I want to buy out those men. How much would it cost?"

"Three or four million. But do you think that that would end the war? They'd take your money and laugh at you."

"Well, dammit, what else can I do?"

"You might end their war."

Martin gaped, "But do you know what they're fighting about?"

"No, and neither does anyone else. But we might be able to arrange this thing."

"See here, Dahlgren, I know you're a good salesman and know the country and all that, but how could one salesman pull two fighting armies apart? That's impossible."

"One salesman couldn't."

"But on the other hand, Dahlgren, if you show me the way, we'll buy all our ships to be used here from Amalgamated. That means a big sale for you."

"Fair enough. Now listen to me, Martin . . ."

A knock sounded at the door and Dahlgren admitted two men. One of them was a small, square-shouldered Chinese gentleman who looked imperially about him. The other was a United States Marine officer named Barnes.

Dahlgren waved them to other chairs. The Chinese preferred to stand and give vent to some of the nervous energy which made him twitch. The Marine was a little bored.

"I've been helping Mr. Kuong locate you, Martin. We've looked all over town."

"Anything serious?" asked Martin.

"No, nothing serious, sir," said Kuong, twisting his high silk hat about, "but I understand that . . . that you were coming to see Mr. Dahlgren and I thought perhaps I could . . . help you just as well."

Dahlgren grinned. "You probably could, Kuong. Perhaps much better."

"Yes, yes. I understood, Mr. Martin, that you wanted to locate a landing field in the Chahar district, in the foothills of the Khinghan Mountains. I . . . I might be able to arrange that for you."

"Splendid!" cried Martin, sitting up very interested. "This is a bit of luck, Dahlgren."

"Is it?" said Dahlgren. "Go on, Kuong."

The Marine was also taking an interest. "That's fine. I was told to help you out, you know. This is a pretty big thing for this country."

"For perhaps a mere million," said Kuong, twisting about and avoiding their eyes, "I might be able to . . ."

"A mere million?" said Dahlgren. "May I ask what connection you would employ to get that field?"

"My methods are above reproach!" cried Kuong. "Must I be insulted by this?"

"Cut it," said the Marine. "A mere million is a lot of dough."

"You were suggesting a plan," said Martin, anxious to change their thoughts.

"Why, yes," replied Dahlgren, easily with a hint of a smile. "My friend Feng-Feng is near here. If I passed the word . . ."

"Hell's bells!" roared the Marine. "You mean Wind-Gone-Mad? Where can I lay my hands on him, huh? Say, that guy has got plenty coming to him, the damned pirate."

"Er, yes," said Martin, "I had heard that this man was not quite within the borders of the law. I . . ."

"There is no law in this country," said Dahlgren. "If you want things done, you must resort to force. As for being a pirate, Wind-Gone-Mad objects to the phrase and the word. He is seeking what you seek, a quiet China."

"Yeah, he sure acts like it," said the Marine. "Scooting around in a pursuit plane, knocking ships out of the sky and bumping off any and everybody he meets on the ground."

"I . . . I don't believe I'd want this chap in on it," said Martin, cautiously.

"If he shows his face to me," cried Kuong, "I'll kill him with my bare hands. Once before he trifled with my business. . . ."

"And you came out second best," replied Dahlgren.

"You're the only friend he has in China," said Kuong, "and for that friendship you will someday pay the toll. In part you are paying it now. Men are suspicious of this friendship. Men do not want to purchase planes from an outlaw's friend."

"I hear," said the Marine, "that he makes the sale and you deliver. That isn't business, that's blackmail. One of these days we'll catch up with your pal, Dahlgren, and it'll be just too bad. And maybe you'll see daylight then—right through him."

Dahlgren got up, lazily. "It isn't such a big job, you know.

Only two armies to fight. Ought to be finished in a week. I guess I'll see if I can find him."

"Don't!" cried Martin, really alarmed by now. "I do not want the stigma of his name attached to this new airline. I'll accept Mr. Kuong's offer!"

"Yes, yes," said Kuong.

Dahlgren reached for his soft felt hat and his topcoat. "You'll be hearing from him, Martin. I'll go north myself just to see what I can see. And to keep tabs on our friend Kuong."

He turned and went out and the Marine stared at Kuong, and Martin stared at the Marine, and Kuong glared at the door.

Chapter Two

TWO days later a scarlet ship rode down through the yellow sky. The earth slid up over the engine cowl at five miles a minute and the roar of the motor drummed against the yellow plain like the roar of a mighty storm.

Wind-Gone-Mad squinted through the silvery arc of the prop. Of his face, only his mouth and nose were visible. A huge pair of goggles adequately masked him, a glass domino. His helmet fit snugly to his head. Upon it, sprawling out with flame-colored scales, a dragon was painted. On the round ear tabs two Chinese characters were printed: "Feng-Feng," meaning hurricane, translated Wind-Gone-Mad.

The blood-steeped javelin of speed was emblazoned with the dragon and the characters. There could be no doubt as to the identity of this man.

The red and ruined monastery doubled and trebled in size. A white sheet against the yellow ground grew from a dot to a large square. But down in that toy town not a soldier could be seen.

"They believed the message," muttered Wind-Gone-Mad with half a smile. "Perhaps Tsing the Fool is not such a fool after all."

He looked back to the south, toward the sharp outline of the Khinghan Mountains. No one followed him. He looked to the east across the undulating drab expanse of waste land. Over there Lee Chang and his glorified bandits would be encamped, perhaps wondering over the message they had received.

The monastery was close under his wings now. He put a tip down and went around like a spiraling gull, silencing his engine. The tipping earth revealed no signs of danger.

Was it possible that Tsing the Fool would surrender so easily to one man? Wind-Gone-Mad had thought it would be otherwise.

Soothed by the whisper of his wires, he relaxed his hands and brought them away from the machine-gun trips. He felt a little let down. He did not think he was well known deep into Mongolia, but here was the evidence.

He decided to let matters rest as they were. Perhaps he would come back at night and talk with Tsing. He was already overdue at the camp of Lee Chang.

He shot the soup to his engine, leveled out and soared upward. The monastery drew away as though falling free. The pilot looked back toward the ground and saw that a soldier stood beside the spread cloth. The soldier was waving his arms, pointing to the white signal and then up toward the sky.

Once more Wind-Gone-Mad went back. They were obviously signaling him to come down. Was Tsing the Fool to be trusted? Wind-Gone-Mad eased back his throttle and glided toward the red walls. The soldier was signaling, holding up empty hands. A man in a blue jacket stood in a doorway also waving. That would be Tsing himself.

Wind-Gone-Mad owed his reputation to the fact that he never passed a dare. He saw a field level enough for a landing. Going around, boosting his engine, he came in for a landing.

He stood up in his pit and made certain that his helmet was buckled and that his goggles were in place. Then, seated upon the turtleback, he waited for the first men to come out.

Tsing the Fool came alone, waddling and wheezing and evidently very much distressed. His ink spots, which he used for eyes, were shifty, but he smiled when he came to a stop.

"Welcome!" cried Tsing the Fool. "You honor us with your visit."

"You've developed a set of manners, Tsing."

"Ah, was I not always a gentleman? Have I ever refused to listen to the wisdom of the Hurricane? May I make you comfortable in our humble camp?"

"Not this time. I have other business to attend to."

"But please do me the small favor of taking some butter and tea. I have much to discuss with you and this place is hardly fitted to be a council chamber for two such great warlords. I wish to know your plans. Perhaps I can help you. I always have been on the side of the right."

"Even in your bandit days, eh?"

"Of course. I helped free an oppressed Mongolia. Come into my camp so that we may talk and take our ease. I hate to stand. I give you my word that you shall go free when we have finished."

Wind-Gone-Mad probed the fat and smiling face. Then he dropped down to the sand beside Tsing and walked with him toward the monastery. Behind them the plane's engine ran itself out. Above them the yellow sky glowed with a strange light. On all sides the plains drifted out into saffron mist.

The monastery appeared deserted. Tsing the Fool led the way through the great square doors and into a small room. The place was littered with cushions and silks and carpets.

Wind-Gone-Mad settled back in a chair and hitched his automatic into a more comfortable position. Tsing the Fool sighed with contentment and sat down.

"Now what is this all about?" said Tsing.

"An airway company needs a field in this region. They cannot have a field here until the country is quiet. You and Lee Chang must bury your quarrel."

"Bury my quarrel with Lee Chang? With that blackguard? Why, my dear Hurricane, my esteemed brother, this Lee Chang is the greatest villain who ever infested this region. He is thin and scaly. He has horrible appetites. He kills his own men but for the fun of it. I am protecting Mongolia against him and I am an honorable warrior. My motives have never been questioned!"

"True, true," said Wind-Gone-Mad, "but what are you two men fighting about?"

"He wants all of Mongolia!" cried Tsing. "He wants it all for himself!"

"And, of course, you want it all for yourself."

"Yes, of course. Ah, he is a wicked man, that Lee Chang. A grasping, cruel devil. Why, do you know that once I went to raid a village along the rails. I went because my men were starving. I went because I had to have money. And what did

I find? The village was in ruins. This Lee Chang had taken every pig, every horse! He had left nothing for me. He had driven the people from their homes! There, you see? He is nothing but a bandit and a bad one at that. He must not be suffered to longer terrorize this district."

"But can't you come to terms?"

"There can be no terms but death between this Lee Chang and me. Too long have I been outraged."

"I think if I talked with Lee Chang, Tsing, I could make him see the light. Supposing I do that thing and come back here and discover what concessions you are willing to make."

"No, no!" cried Tsing, quickly. "Do not scorn my hospitality, poor as it is."

Wind-Gone-Mad rose to his feet. "I cannot take the time and for that I am sorry."

"But you can!" cried Tsing, laughing and standing up. "Chu! Throw back the drapery!"

Wind-Gone-Mad crouched forward, hand flashing to the butt of the .45. But before he could draw, the silks whipped aside and disclosed the blue snout of a machine gun. Chu sat behind it, squinting down the sights. Soldiers stepped out from their concealment along the walls.

"You must stay," said Tsing, bowing humbly. "As my guest. Perhaps you have forgotten an ill turn you once did me, Hurricane. I am not interested in who you are. I am merely interested in killing you. Men, escort this worthy guest to his room while I devise some method of using him as befits his station."

Wind-Gone-Mad stood up straight and dropped his hand.

He was smiling at Tsing and Tsing was laughing. The soldiers, keeping at a respectful distance, escorted Wind-Gone-Mad from the room, the somber light flashing from their fixed bayonets.

They were afraid to touch him. Wind-Gone-Mad could sense that. They allowed him to enter the cell by himself and when the door thundered shut upon him he heard them walk quickly away.

He stood for some little while in the center of the floor, staring out the small square window. The cell had once housed a yellow-robed Lama monk. Its sole furniture was a prayer wheel now fallen into decay. But it still turned and the paper tags which were prayers rattled like dead bones in the drum.

"Om mani padme hum," said Wind-Gone-Mad. "Jewel of the lotus flower." He gave the drum another spin, idly sending several thousand Lama prayers up into the yellow sky.

"Who's that?" said a voice nearby in English.

Wind-Gone-Mad looked about him and saw nothing. "Who calls?"

"Christ! You're an American!"

"Correct," said Wind-Gone-Mad.

"I'm a mining engineer. My name's Bill McCall. What are you doing here?"

Wind-Gone-Mad irreverently stood up on the prayer wheel and peered over the partition of the cell. His gaudy helmet and glinting goggles made the other gasp.

"You're . . . but you can't be! Hell, man, are you the one they call Hurricane?"

"That's right. What are you doing here?"

McCall shook his tousled blond head dolefully. "They caught me on the trail. I was trying to make Kalgan. But I didn't have any dust on me so they don't know about it."

"Dust? There's plenty of dust in this country."

"I mean gold dust. I've got to get out of here. I can't work the place anymore. Since this war started no coolies will stick to me. If they do, they die. But Tsing doesn't know about the dust. He thinks I'm after tin. Lee Chang hasn't come near me. Oh, Lord, why did I ever come into this country? I've been here a month and if I don't get to Peking in three days, I'm washed up."

"What are you talking about?" said Wind-Gone-Mad.

The engineer stood up and looked long at the glinting goggles. The engineer was young, about twenty-four. He was dressed in whipcord breeches and laced boots and a flannel shirt. His face was sorrow-stamped and his smoky eyes hopeless.

"I've got a mine up here about thirty miles and there's plenty of the old rock there. Lord knows just how much. Millions most likely. Oxide ore. They didn't savvy oxide ore. Cyanide mining, you understand. I've got a lot blocked out and surveyed. My control's run about half a million already. Enough for machinery.

"Gold's where you find it, you know. I found this. There's a little salt lake right beside the mine. Plenty of water. I've been monkeying with cyaniding and I've got about a hundred grand out already, but I was afraid to carry it to Peking with me. I wanted to get some soldiers down there. Maybe the Nanking government would do something about it when I fixed up my concession papers a second time. I've got to fix them up again, you know, and then the mine will belong to me.

"But I guess I can't do anything about it now. I can't get to Peking in three days. I've tried to buy myself out of here, but if I told Tsing I had the jack, I'd be working for him the rest of my life. My option's up, you see, and I can't go on unless I get it renewed in three days. You understand now?"

"Yes. I understand."

"But you're Wind-Gone-Mad. I've heard about you down in Central China. I heard about that dragon and I can read the name on the ear tabs. I heard a plane a while ago and I thought maybe somebody had come up to look for me. But they wouldn't do that. They aren't interested in me. Nobody is."

"Maybe I am."

"Say, do you mean it? Say, listen, if you could get this thing straight for me you could have half of the mine. Honest-to-God, you could."

"Three days," said Wind-Gone-Mad, thoughtfully rocking back and forth on the prayer wheel. "That's not much time to lick two armies and get you to Peking. But I guess I can do it all right."

"But, holy smoke, you're in jail, just like me. And there isn't any way out of it. What'd you do to Tsing?"

"I tripped up a war of his once. He didn't like it. Right now he's down there trying to figure out how much he'll get for me in blood money. I'm worth quite a bit, they say. And a poor warlord like Tsing would hardly pass up such a chance. If he sends my corpse to Peking, he can't send it to Mukden, and if he turns me over to Nanking, the Shanghai bankers won't pay up. He's got to know just how much money he's going to get."

"Ugh!" said McCall.

"But at the same time he's afraid to shoot me because his soldiers think it would be bad luck."

Boots clattered and sandals scuffed the stone pavement outside. Rifles thudded to the floor. The door swung back to disclose Tsing in all the glory of his blue silk jacket. Tsing was laughing silently and his cheeks bounced in time with his paunch.

"Ho, ho, but you thought I would go back on my promise not to detain you, eh? I had you worried that time. I suppose you thought I was going to kill you, eh?"

"I suppose so," said Wind-Gone-Mad.

"Well, I wasn't going to do that, not after I happened to think of something I found out yesterday. Did you know I was going to have a pilot and plane up here by tomorrow?"

"No, are you?"

"Yes, certainly. And yesterday, two pilots and planes arrived for Lee Chang. Oh, I know everything. I even knew you were coming before that message arrived from you. I know everything!"

"That's dandy," said Wind-Gone-Mad. "But what am I supposed to do?"

"Now my plane won't be here until tomorrow and this is early in the afternoon. Lee Chang might want to bomb me or something of the sort and so I think it best that you go over and kill his pilots. How do you like that?"

"Fine, but how . . ."

"Hurricane, I know your weakness. I know the weakness of any foreign devil. They do not want to think that they have caused the death of a countryman. Now in the cell next to yours—" He stopped to laugh again. "In the cell next to yours, there is a young American who has been doing some silly digging up to the north of here. Should you fail to come back, then, poo! The young American dies. It is as simple as that.

"And if you do come back, then I am afraid I shall have to let you go again. I am very softhearted, Hurricane."

"I've noticed that."

"Now you see how well I plan? You come in here, talk to this young man, you feel sorry for him. Now I know you will return. As a reward for coming back I will let this young man go free, perhaps. All you must do is kill those pilots. They are nobodies. Mercenary fools. Then when my plane comes, I shall have the upper hand with no risk to myself whatever."

"Where did you get this information?"

Tsing the Fool laughed again and shook his head. "Ask no questions. We have gasoline for your plane and bullets for your guns. Come, we send you into the skies with our blessing."

The red ship's dragons spat fire from the exhaust stacks, the engine howled like a thousand demons, and Wind-Gone-Mad charged across the desert sky into the east, toward the camp of Lee Chang.

The sun was low and where a caravan crawled the shadows of the camels stood out in black streaks. Each rock had a shadow ten times its size, each house spread its black rectangle far across the yellow sands below the yellow sky.

"And so," said Wind-Gone-Mad, "they are going to have

pilots now. Odd coincidence when they never thought of having them before. But Blakely doesn't care what he sells or where he sells it."

No, Demming Aircraft didn't care. A sale was a sale, and here in these turbulent days of Japanese conquest it was difficult to foretell how arms would be used. Sleek-haired Blakely was far in the south, so thought Wind-Gone-Mad. Sleek-haired Blakely had every reason to stay out of the north, far from Wind-Gone-Mad.

Planes for the glorified bandits. That was a mistake. Neither Lee Chang nor Tsing the Fool should have planes at their call. The country was unsettled and beleaguered enough without that. Jim Dahlgren had once been offered a contract from Peking and the terms had been vague. The man named Kuong had thought that a few ships could keep Mongolia quiet. Bandits were getting bad, Kuong had said, and a man's interests were not safe.

Wind-Gone-Mad wondered what Kuong might have meant by his "interests." Kuong's interests were notoriously bad.

He spotted a huddle of buildings a little to the south: Lee Chang's headquarters. The Mongol operated from here, inconsistently pillaging the countryside, robbing caravans and boasting that he fought for the freedom of his land, even as Tsing the Fool.

Lee Chang could do without planes very well. He could only obtain renegade pilots, thanks to his reputation.

To buy the life of one with the death of two was everyday business in China, too common to remark in Manchuria, unnoticed in Mongolia.

He listened to the yowl of his hundreds of horses and wondered about the kid named Bill McCall. If the country had enough Bill McCalls, it would quiet itself in no time.

Lee Chang's camp sprang into action at the first sound of the engine's snarl. Men streamed out of the huts, dragging machine guns into place, swiveling rapid-fire artillery and aiming it at the skies.

But the two planes were not in evidence. Could Tsing have been mistaken?

At five miles a minute, Wind-Gone-Mad rolled distance under his retracted gear. At twenty-seven hundred feet per second, machine-gun bullets ascended spitefully into the yellow sky.

Wind-Gone-Mad stared down at the huts spiraling, unwilling to open fire before he knew definitely about the planes. Holes appeared in his tail surfaces. Daylight leaped through his wings.

The sun sank into a red ball of flame and spun on top of the misty horizon. The world turned scarlet.

Sparks ribboned out through the prop arc. Lead stabbed into the huts, passed through the gun crews, raced on in a straight, cleaving line of dust geysers. The red ship vaulted skyward and came about.

Wind-Gone-Mad looked about the jumping, weaving horizon for a sign of the two planes which might be here. He caught sight of a black dot against the mist of red. The fighter was coming fast.

Evidently, thought the man called Feng-Feng, Lee Chang

was already using the ships for the purpose of banditry. That would have to be stopped.

The black dot became larger. In the gathering twilight, gaudy flowers bloomed through the propeller. Wind-Gone-Mad came around in a wingover to meet the charge of the enemy plane.

Not until then did the Chinese pilot see the device of the dragon, but even that did not make him sheer off. With doubled fury, the Chinese sent his craft hurtling up to meet the other.

Wind-Gone-Mad dived down and then up, zooming straight for the belly of the black pursuit plane. Tracer bit into fabric. Streamers lanced back and fluttered from the trailing edge of the other's wing.

The red ship went over on its back. Upside down, at five miles a minute, Wind-Gone-Mad pressed his trips. The yellow face was staring back. The black ship was yawing.

He knew the pilot then. It was a renegade named Rauski, a man who had met Wind-Gone-Mad before. And then the tracer bit.

The black ship careened up on one wing and fell off, engine yowling a death chant through the ugly dusk, smoke pouring from the cowl.

Instantly, Wind-Gone-Mad was deluged with splinters from his cowl. He kicked rudder, came about and stared into the sunset. Another black plane was upon him. Wind-Gone-Mad slid out of the way, went into a vertical, and with engine full on, fell in with this second killer.

Rauski's plane crashed with a flare of red and showered sparks for a hundred yards about it. With that for an example, the second pilot had no thought of giving battle. He dived steeply for the ground, passing into the machine gun area above the huts.

Wind-Gone-Mad, facing that updriving sheet of lead, held a steady stick. The other ship's elevators flashed through his ringsight. With a quick burst, Wind-Gone-Mad shot them away.

A parachute spanked into a hemisphere of white. The other pilot drifted away from his plummeting craft. Machine-gun bullets chewed great holes in Wind-Gone-Mad's wings.

The red ship zoomed the huts and lanced out toward the darkening plains. Behind, the machine guns fell silent. The crackle of two ships burning filled the air.

Wind-Gone-Mad, using the last ray of dying daylight, picked out a landing field and slid down toward the dark ground. His wheels crunched the sand and his ship bucked to a stop.

He climbed down and wiped flecks of blood from his jaw where the splinters had struck. He sat for a long time in the darkness, thinking matters out.

He did not feel badly about downing two ships. He would have had to do it sooner or later anyway. Lee Chang would have put them to good use in pillaging this country. No man could have avoided Lee Chang's thin, grasping hand as long as that hand held two planes.

The problem which now confronted Wind-Gone-Mad was not so easy to solve. He knew he stood no chance in actually beating these men down by force. They had too many gray-coated soldiers for that, and even if they were beaten it would not guarantee that they would stay beaten.

Panama-Pacific wanted their field. The American kid had to get to Peking to save his concession. But Wind-Gone-Mad knew that if he returned to Tsing's camp, Tsing would forget all about his promises.

Lee Chang lay at ease upon his bed, dusty boots carelessly soiling the silken cover, opium pipe sending its stench throughout the hut. His narrow, dried face was rapt with dreaming. He was visualizing himself in a gaudy uniform, standing with his boot on Tsing the Fool's neck, saying, "Off with his head!"

It was a lovely dream, but an ugly memory jarred it and made it fade. Two sleek pursuit planes were still hot in the sands. One pilot lived, but that was a minor consolation. The plane was the thing.

Lee Chang propped himself on his elbow and fumbled thoughtfully with his nose. His gray tunic was unbuttoned at the throat and some stray bits of food were scattered on the pocket flaps. He scratched his bald head and probed under his arm for fleas. A cruel light flickered in his close-set eyes, a wicked leer was stamped on his drooping mouth.

He rolled and lit another pellet, inhaling deeply. Then he sprawled at his ease again and dreamed that he had a boot on the neck of one called Wind-Gone-Mad. "Off with his head!" bawled Lee Chang.

The thought so enraged him that he sat bolt upright and

slammed his pipe against the wall, breaking it. He glared at the pieces and then leaped to his feet. "May the fiends of hell rip him asunder! May the dogs gnaw on his putrid flesh!"

The guards at the door looked in, startled. Lee Chang flung himself upon them, kicking them. "Out of my sight! Fools. You stood there not an hour ago and let him escape! Fools! You let him steal our two planes! Get out!"

The two guards ran away, glad to leave their night's vigil. Lee Chang threw himself down upon his bed again and fumbled for his opium pipe. But the pipe was broken and his anger mounted until his head felt like a caldron of hell broth.

He rolled over and faced the wall, muttering filth and scratching his fleas. After a while he realized that the wind no longer entered the room and the burning lamp was low.

He sat up suddenly and stayed there, stiff with surprise. He gripped the bedpost to support himself.

Wind-Gone-Mad sat serenely across the room fondling Lee Chang's sword. The door was shut and the blinds were closed. The smoky yellow light from the lamp glittered on the goggles. The dragon looked like a river of blood running down the helmet. The mouth smiled with half a smile.

"I think," said Wind-Gone-Mad, "that I had better kill you."

Lee Chang turned from yellow to gray and looked at the shining sword which rested nakedly in Wind-Gone-Mad's hands.

"And if you open your mouth to yell, I will," added Wind-Gone-Mad, quietly. "Didn't you receive my warning?"

"Ah . . . ah . . . yes, yes."

"Then why did you give orders to shoot at me?"

74

"I . . . it . . . it was all a mistake."

"Yes, so I see. You know, my better judgment keeps telling me that you should die. It would be a very simple thing to run this sword through you and out the other side and then pin your body to the wall for your men to see."

"No, no!"

"Oh, yes, yes. But I have a feeling that your death would mean nothing."

"Of course not."

"Because one of your men would step in and carry on the fight just the same. No, I had better not run you through, but you had better do as I say."

"Command me!" begged Lee Chang, shivering and shrinking into himself.

"Stop this war with Tsing the Fool."

"Oh, but I cannot. Tsing boasts that he will kill me and all my men. Tsing wants all of Mongolia to himself."

"And so you want it for yourself."

"Yes, yes. I . . . must have it. There is one who tells me what Tsing means to do."

"And who is that?"

"Even under the pain of death I could not divulge his name."

"No, of course not. You won't break off this war?"

"I cannot."

"Then why don't you go and whip Tsing right now? He does not expect it." Wind-Gone-Mad lowered the sword point to the earthen floor and began to carve out rectangles. Lee Chang forgot his fleas as he watched the design.

"This," said Wind-Gone-Mad, "is the plan of the monastery.

An attack here would be easy. The guns are here . . . and here . . . and here. The defenses are not adequate here . . . and here."

"Is this true?"

"Has Wind-Gone-Mad ever lied to you?"

"No . . . but I thought it was otherwise at Tsing's base."

"Not a bit of it. Attack there about dawn and you can kill every man in Tsing's command."

Lee Chang's eyes glittered craftily. He licked his scaly lips. "Every man?"

"Yes, of course. And now, in return for this information, suppose you furnish me with a horse."

Hope gleamed in Lee Chang's brittle face. This was his chance to call the guard. He went to the door and cried, "Captain Shen! Bring me a horse."

Boots thudded outside. Hoofs clattered. Saddle leather creaked. And then Lee Chang, having a dozen armed men outside, whirled and bawled, "Wind-Gone-Mad! Take him, you fools! Take him!"

Soldiers rushed into the room, sabers drawn, pistols ready. They halted and looked inquiringly at Lee Chang and then knowingly at the opium pipe and each other.

Wind-Gone-Mad had vanished.

Around the borders of the lake lay a fringe of hard-packed salty sand, left there by the unreplenished water which had receded through the centuries. From five thousand feet, against the blue-white brilliance of the cold moon, Wind-Gone-Mad had little difficulty in locating a landing runway.

It was close to midnight and all good Mongols slept, even when they heard a drumming in the sky. The southern fringe of the Shamo desert was as ghostly as a cemetery and the mountains rose flatly here and there, like tombstones.

With silenced engine, Wind-Gone-Mad drifted down and dropped a parachute flare just to make certain that the runway was without obstruction. He bounced to a stop and stood up. As far as he could see the white reaches stretched.

His problem was a simple one. He had only to look for a cluster of shacks up against a hill and he would find Bill McCall's mine.

From the war box at his back he took a pair of fine night glasses and examined the knoll close beside the lake. He saw huts against the brown cliff.

Still standing he eased off his brakes and shot the throttle up the trident. But the ship would not taxi straight and he had to put his feet on the rudders.

Presently the plane was crouched in the shadow of the knoll. All was silent. The gloomy buildings leaned against one another as though for support.

Higher up the hill stood a stone structure, obviously a ruined temple forgotten even by the Lama priests.

Wind-Gone-Mad shut off his engine and poked through the huts. Bill McCall, in spite of opposition, had gone quite far in his preparation of the mine. He had a few tools of the cruder sort. He had rigged a stamp mill with an old automobile engine and he had a riffle box made from tiles taken out of the temple.

Wind-Gone-Mad located a few drums of gasoline and a

piece of chamois and managed to replenish his fuel supply. Then he went back up the hill toward the temple. The building was cold and austere by moonlight, hugging great shadows to its walls. The curved roof line swooped and turned against the sky.

Stabbing a flashlight ahead of him, Wind-Gone-Mad saw that the place was still livable. In fact, a pile of duffle in the great hall attested that Bill McCall had used this for his office.

A machinery crate stood in the center of the floor, littered with papers. That was McCall's desk. Satisfied, Wind-Gone-Mad made certain that the place had but one entrance. As he lashed the white beam of light through the room, he saw two sour-faced gods in the last stages of decay. They were mounted upon a dais, looking straight at him unblinking even though the light was bright.

So Bill McCall, a product of the restless West, had worked in company with these two ageless Eastern gods who sat silent for centuries.

"Om mani padme hum," said Wind-Gone-Mad, and promptly remembered that if he failed to return, Bill McCall would pay for that failure with his life.

Wind-Gone-Mad poked through the buildings again, finally unearthing the dynamite cache. He shouldered a box of the red-wrapped sticks and carried them to his plane. Then he added a keg of blasting powder and finally came back for caps and fuse, knowing better than to carry them with the dynamite itself.

All this safely stowed in the compartment at his back, he

turned about and taxied over the rough and jolting ground until he could swing into the wind.

The moon danced in the lake and remained aloof in the sky. The motor roared like a thousand Lama bull fiddles tortured all together. Wind-Gone-Mad smiled with half his mouth and spurred his ship toward the camp of Tsing the Fool.

The dawn pasted a strip of dirty gray across the east. The wind awoke and began to sob through the brooding red monastery. A sentry yawned at his post in the tower and then stood up straight with a quick jerk of his rifle.

"Who's there?"

Only the weeping of the wind.

"Who's there?" cried the sentry, fear of the unknown shaking him.

The footstep came again. Not loud, but enough. Through the misty dimness a shadow drifted. A stone rattled out on the plain. The sentry whirled to face this new menace.

The soft slap of a handkerchief wrapped rock was not loud. The sentry sank down under the battlements. In a moment he was tied with his own rifle sling and bandolier.

Wind-Gone-Mad stood up from the work and looked about him. In the other tower, the bound figure was barely discernible in the gloom.

Scrambling down the outside of the squat watchtower, he went to work on the side of the building. The rasping grate of a drill and the tap of a hammer were loud, but he could not help that.

Finishing at that place, he went around to another side of the monastery. He worked against the rising sun and when he had finished, yellow fingers of daylight were probing the compound.

With a satisfied nod he turned away and slipped down the wall, intent on escape before the men were up and about. He rounded a corner and walked straight into the waiting arms of Captain Chu.

Wind-Gone-Mad dodged. Steel slithered as Chu whipped out his saber. The Chinese officer lunged, face tight with effort, slanted eyes glittering with the lust to kill.

The point passed through the skirt of Wind-Gone-Mad's leather jacket. Wind-Gone-Mad whirled to the right, wrenching the caught saber from Chu's hand.

Chu started to cry out, but before his lips could open, Wind-Gone-Mad whipped up the saber, gripping the point, and slammed the hilt against the side of Chu's head.

Chu melted into the dust. Wind-Gone-Mad replaced the saber in its scabbard and crept noiselessly toward the door of the monastery. He went slowly, looking for sentries in the courtyards.

A gray jacket detached itself from the shadows. Wind-Gone-Mad pressed against the rough wall. The soldier, walking sluggishly, passed within a yard of Wind-Gone-Mad without seeing him. He went on outside.

Wind-Gone-Mad grinned. He cat-footed across the paving and found Tsing the Fool's quarters. He was about to open the door when he heard a footstep close beside him. They were changing the guard.

Stooping quickly, Wind-Gone-Mad picked up a pebble and shied it at the decayed statue of a helmeted war dog.

*The Chinese officer lunged, face tight with effort,
slanted eyes glittering with the lust to kill.*

A gasp greeted the sharp crack. The sentry turned about and ran toward the figure.

Wind-Gone-Mad slipped into Tsing's bedroom and closed the door quietly behind him.

Tsing was sprawled on a low divan, mouth open, bloated with sleep. Wind-Gone-Mad looked cheerfully about him and tore down a silken drapery.

This he wadded and then, holding the thing before him, approached the couch. With a sudden lunge he gagged Tsing and threw the rest of the drapery about the gross body.

Tsing struggled, trying to come awake. His eyes opened sleepily and angrily and then shot wider. Wind-Gone-Mad stood over him, goggles throwing back the rays of sunlight which stabbed through the window.

"Quick! You have no time to lose!" said Wind-Gone-Mad. "Lee Chang is coming here with all his troops!"

"Blug!" said Tsing, struggling to get up.

"Somehow he found a map of your fortifications. He knows just where to attack. Meet him on the open plain. You have little time, you must march immediately. I downed his two ships and I have come back. Our bargain is completed."

"Gurk," said Tsing.

Wind-Gone-Mad knelt and lashed the ends of the drapery to the couch. "You'll have men in here to free you in about five minutes. Lee Chang is boasting that he'll kill your forces to a man."

Wind-Gone-Mad went to the door and swung it open a fraction of an inch. The sentry was leaning against it. Flinging the door back, throwing the sentry off balance,

Wind-Gone-Mad reached out and jerked the sentry into the room. Another drapery floated to the floor and the sentry was securely bound and gagged.

Wind-Gone-Mad stepped into the courtyard. Voices buzzed outside. It would be impossible to escape. He turned and ran toward the rear of the building.

A few minutes later an excited voice sent a string of commands out across the compound. Soldiers stopped in their tracks looking about them, surprised.

Captain Chu, supported by the two men who had found him, was dragged into sight. "He is here! The devil is here!" cried Chu. "Scatter and find him! Rouse Tsing. Move, you lice!"

Soldiers milled about, some running, some walking, some merely turning. Presently, Tsing, purple of face and awesome in his rage, rushed out of the monastery screaming commands.

The other soldiers were discovered. A detachment of cavalry went out to scour the plains. Tsing stood in the center of the compound and stamped his feet, sending the dust rolling away from him.

"It's too flat for him to get away. We'll find him. We'll crucify him to the monastery door!"

Minutes went by. The searchers began to straggle in, shaking their heads and lifting their eyebrows by way of explanation. Tsing gradually cooled down until he remembered what Wind-Gone-Mad had said.

Turning to a trumpeter, Tsing shot out a volley of orders. The trumpet's clear notes floated across the plains. Men stirred in the huts and tents. Horses plunged.

The trumpet blared again. Men drew up in companies.

Tsing, mounted upon a rearing black horse gave a final command.

Dust rolled, feet tramped in rhythm. Guns rattled. The great shroud of dust marked the passage of the army.

A few minutes later Bill McCall heard a man walking up a narrow flight of steps. Bill McCall's face was strained and white. He knew that Tsing had gone and that the camp was deserted and he would be deserted and left to starve. No one had come for him or remembered him.

Those footsteps might mean anything. And then Bill McCall drew a long breath. A pair of goggles appeared in the small door port. Wind-Gone-Mad grinned and rattled a set of keys.

"Gee, golly, I thought you were never coming back. What's all this about? What did you do?"

Wind-Gone-Mad smiled. "Started a war. Come on, youngster. The camp is deserted. Not even a sentry left. Maybe we can find something to eat. We've got some waiting to do."

"But won't those guys come back?"

"Maybe, but we've got to wait all the same."

At nine o'clock a speck appeared in the sultry sky and a plane's motor racketed across the plains. Wind-Gone-Mad stood up from his post in the watch tower and turned to Bill McCall.

"Here's our chance. Take this rifle and watch yourself."

"What're you going to do?"

"I'm going to interview this pilot, and if he makes any foolish move, knock him off."

"But who is he?" insisted McCall.

"A new recruit for Tsing's outfit. I'm going to tell him where he can find Tsing."

Wind-Gone-Mad unloosened an automatic in its holster at his side and went down the curving steps to the ground. McCall followed him at a respectful distance.

The plane went around into the wind and settled slowly. It floated halfway across the parade ground and then slammed to earth blowing up great clouds of yellow dust. Wind-Gone-Mad began to run.

Before the dust had cleared, Wind-Gone-Mad was up against the side of the ship, automatic resting on the cowl.

The Chinese pilot's eyes widened. He thrust up his goggles and gasped. "Where . . . where is Tsing?"

"Tsing's busy right now, fighting a war. You're late."

"Who . . . by the devils! You're *Feng-Feng*!"

"That's right. Now get out slowly and don't try anything."

But the Chinese saw death yawning for him whatever he did. He flung himself forward, thrusting the muzzle out of the way, grabbing for his own gun.

Wind-Gone-Mad grabbed the fellow's throat and dragged him headfirst out of the ship, setting him upright in the dust.

"Quit it," said Wind-Gone-Mad. "You're not going to die. I have a use for this two-seater, that's all."

The pilot glared. "I'm not going to give it up."

"Oh, yes, you are. You're going to go out and locate Tsing and tell him that I took his ship. That's the message. Give him my compliments. Beat it."

He threw the Chinese away from him. The man walked

slowly, looking back. Wind-Gone-Mad fired a shot into the dust between the retreating feet. It was more than the Chinese could stand. He ran swiftly out toward the indicated battle ground and disappeared in a wash.

McCall ran out. "What's up?"

"We'll re-gas this ship and get away from here. My pursuit plane is safe. It won't carry two but this one will. Come on."

With the gas tank full and with certain supplies stowed in the rear pit, they headed into the wind and took off, leaving the red monastery far behind them.

McCall looked down at the earth and grinned. Wind-Gone-Mad grinned back.

"Demming doesn't make a bad ship," said Wind-Gone-Mad to himself. "Wait until Blakely hears about this."

His smile broadened. Generally speaking it sounded pretty big to down one airforce and capture another.

They spotted the pilot down below. The man stopped and shook his fist at them. Wind-Gone-Mad zoomed the Chinese and gave him a mock salute.

They flew for several minutes before they spotted Tsing's troops crawling like lead soldiers against the yellow carpet of the earth.

Tsing, in the van, waved triumphantly at them. What Tsing didn't know, thought the pilot, wouldn't hurt him.

The ship roared on toward the stronghold of Lee Chang. Several miles from the fortifications, Lee Chang's troops were hastily digging in and preparing an ambush for the advancing troops of Tsing the Fool. Somehow Lee Chang had gotten word that Tsing was advancing.

"It's going to be a fine war," murmured Wind-Gone-Mad.

Presently they sighted the huts and barracks of Lee Chang's camp. Wind-Gone-Mad had hoped to find the place deserted, but he was disappointed to see at least a company of men wandering about the compound.

He signed to McCall that they were about to land. McCall nodded. The ship sailed downward on whistling wings toward an open space near the huts.

Men came running toward them even before they had stopped. Wind-Gone-Mad threw on the engine, picked up the tail and squeezed the trips.

The machine guns were firing high. The plane charged through the clouds of yellow dust toward the soldiers.

Men scattered. The plane went through them, ground looped, dashed back, ground looped and charged again.

It was too much for the Chinese. They broke and ran, throwing away their weapons to increase their speed.

Wind-Gone-Mad taxied up to the huts again and jumped out. From the rear cockpit he took dynamite and blasting powder and caps. McCall, with a grin of understanding, picked up boxes and carried them at a run toward the buildings.

They heaped the explosive upon the floor of Lee Chang's hut. They found cartridge cases and added them to the pile. They found a stack of aerial bombs provided for the deceased planes.

It made an imposing mound. McCall tamped the cap with his teeth and applied the fuse. Wind-Gone-Mad went around the shack and pounded all the windows shut.

A roaring sound came from the plains. Wind-Gone-Mad

stared at an advancing squadron of cavalry which was backed by rolling dust from infantry. Lee Chang was retreating.

"Go on and fight, you yellow belly," said Wind-Gone-Mad.

McCall struck a match. The fuse sputtered. The pair raced back toward their ship.

But the cavalry had already spotted them. Lances extended, pennons fluttering, troopers in gray charged to get between the two and the plane.

Wind-Gone-Mad looked hopelessly back at the huts. He jerked out his automatic and fired at the front rank before them. He dropped on one knee and emptied a clip.

He tried to jam a second clip into the gun. Lances were pointing down at him, hoofs thundered, a concerted yell of victory came from a score of yellow throats.

Wind-Gone-Mad stood his ground. He aimed and emptied a saddle. He stood bolt upright like a duelist waiting for the fatal bullet. His mouth was set in a firm line. His hands did not shake. The glinting goggles stared full at death and remained unafraid.

The gray avalanche roared forward. Lances gleamed. Sabers slashed in anticipation.

Behind them, not far away, a fuse sputtered across an earthen floor toward a pile of munitions and dynamite and powder, enough to tear down a city.

Boots planted firmly, Wind-Gone-Mad emptied another saddle. The world was a churning mass of hoofs and yellow faces and glittering steel. Less than fifty feet separated him from the charging front rank.

A machine gun racketed savagely above the din. A motor

roared. Horses in the rear rank skidded and crashed to earth, pitching their riders under grinding hoofs.

The front rank wheeled. The machine gun came nearer. Wind-Gone-Mad stood astonished, watching the plane charge the cavalry.

Troopers screamed and applied spur. The squadron dashed helter-skelter out of the way. Wind-Gone-Mad raced forward toward the ship.

Bill McCall was standing in the rear cockpit behind the double guns. He eased back the auxiliary throttle with a grin.

"Thanks," said Wind-Gone-Mad, and climbed into the front pit.

The ship gathered speed and launched itself into the air. Behind them a thunderous roar sent them soaring and skidding wildly.

Wind-Gone-Mad looked back. Lee Chang's camp erupted into a geyser of flame. Masonry and dirt, supply wagons, roofs, tents, artillery, all shot upward toward the sullen sky.

Splinters rained for the space of a minute and when the dust had begun to clear, Lee Chang's camp was in shambles.

"Now fight!" yelled Wind-Gone-Mad into the slipstream.

Tsing's army had drawn back at the sound of the explosion. Tsing sat on his black horse and stared at the dark cloud which hovered over the shattered post. Tsing was not laughing now.

Lee Chang's ambush was not far from Tsing, but Lee Chang had forgotten all about the ambush. Lee Chang's men streamed out of their entrenchments and looked dazedly east.

Tsing laughed and whirled to his trumpeter. "Sound charge!"

Tsing's troops dashed forward. Lee Chang's men dropped

back into concealment. Machine guns started up. Cannons rumbled. The spiteful crackle of rifle fire split through the uproar.

Column on column of men poured into the raging fire of Lee Chang. But Lee Chang's men were unnerved, lacking a second line to fall back into.

Men came to grips in the dust. Bayonets flamed in the sunlight and then flamed red.

Above the din of the battle came the roar of a motor. Machine guns lashed out of the skies. Face after face turned up to meet this new menace.

"Hurrah!" cried Tsing. "He's with me!"

The ship hammered Lee Chang's lines into rubbish. Men vaulted out of their trenches and scattered before the withering strafe.

And then the plane came around and dived straight at the forces of Tsing.

Men gaped, unable to understand what had happened. But Wind-Gone-Mad sat behind his jarring machine guns and swept everything out of his path.

"Wind-Gone-Mad!" screamed Tsing in sudden understanding.

The plane yowled up again and came back. Soldiers scattered, diving behind rocks, running, trying to get away with no thought of fighting back.

Lee Chang's men and Tsing's troops were becoming entangled. Both armies were dressed in gray. It was impossible to tell which was which.

The melee spread into a panic. A soldier of Lee Chang ran

side by side with a soldier of Tsing and they had no thought of killing—they craved only life.

Wind-Gone-Mad drew off. He scribbled upon a pad, attached the note to an empty machine-gun drum and tossed it down in the path of the fleeing Tsing.

Going back, Wind-Gone-Mad wrote a similar note to Lee Chang and dropped it into a group of running men. They threw themselves down, thinking it was a bomb, but presently they crawled back to inspect it.

Then Wind-Gone-Mad flew west at full throttle until the red monastery loomed up against the ground. He turned to McCall. McCall was white of face and somewhat puzzled, but he nodded.

Wind-Gone-Mad slacked off his throttle. "You've got the bomb toggles back there. Hit the monastery!"

He dived low over the squat red building. McCall pulled the releases one after the other. No bomb hit the building, but suddenly it blasted apart with sheets of flame, knocking the plane high into the air with concussion.

The towers fell in upon each other. The red dust of the masonry rose up in a scarlet shroud. Tsing's camp was a shambles, and from afar, Tsing saw the explosion and heard the ground tremble. Tsing shook his fist.

Wind-Gone-Mad rocketed into the north, toward the lake which sparkled in the sunlight. The salt-packed earth shimmered. The mine buildings slept.

Wind-Gone-Mad landed and came in close to the cluster of huts.

"Say," said McCall, "I didn't hit that. . . ."

"I know. I drilled it with dynamite and blasting powder and set the caps between the stones. It went blooey when your bombs hit close to it."

"But gee, that's a clean sweep, isn't it?"

"Not on your life," said Wind-Gone-Mad. "They'll be right back at it again and we'll have gained nothing, unless . . ."

"Unless what?"

"Listen, McCall, you sit tight here. We're forty miles from Tsing and Lee Chang. With that outfit they can't make the trip in anything less than twelve hours. I'll be back by that time. I left my own ship cached up in those hills, about fifteen miles from here. I went from there to Tsing's camp in a commandeered cart. But I've got to go to Peking. I'll be back before you know it."

"But my concessions!"

"You won't have any concession unless I do the thing this way. I think I know all about it by now. Sit tight."

Bill McCall waited through the day. When dusk came across the craggy mountains and dropped a curtain on the stretches of sand and gravel, he took his place in the top of the temple tower and sat on a battlement, listening to the silence of the mine.

He took the night glasses Wind-Gone-Mad had given him and from time to time he studied the dim horizon, watching for the return of the ship.

He did not understand Wind-Gone-Mad's plans, but he had faith in them. Something about the pilot inspired faith. Hadn't the man thrown two armies into disruption? Hadn't he blown up the two camps? Yes, he merited faith.

McCall looked down at the silent buildings below him. It had taken a long time to build up this mine to a point where it could be worked. God knew how many millions were stowed away in this mountain waiting for his drills and stamps.

Six months before he had tried to get a permanent concession from the powers that be. They had listened to him politely and had told him that if he could show them the proof at the end of the year, they would grant him what he wanted.

But six months' work had been little enough and he had gone into the labor with a will. And then his coolies had begun to leave him. Men had been murdered. Shots had come from the darkness.

Still, no personal danger had been apparent and McCall had worked on by himself. And then these two armies had moved into the region and that had been the end of all work. What had been done, had been done by his two hands. But he had the proof for the powers that be. He could show them yellow gold. That would be enough.

For ten percent of the gross they would give him all the guards and labor he needed.

McCall sat up suddenly. It was close to midnight and the moon had risen, sending its curved blade across the water. From far off came the clank and clatter of men and arms.

He took up the night glasses and the moonlight showed him two columns of troops marching side by side, heading straight for the mine.

Restlessly, McCall studied the sky and listened for the sound of an engine. But aside from the noise of the soldiers, the skies were still.

Would he be trapped in this place, defenseless? Wind-Gone-Mad should have returned before this. McCall dragged a rifle up to his side. Well, they'd have a hell of a time taking him, anyway.

Minutes dragged out. The two snaky columns of black on the salty plain came nearer. McCall waited with the wind in his blond hair.

And then his heart began to beat again. A far-off drumming came faintly to him. He stood up, grinning. In a moment he picked out the plane.

The two columns of troops suddenly split apart and scuttled for cover, but the plane soared on, paying them no heed. The two-seater coasted in for a landing before the mine huts.

Wind-Gone-Mad jumped out, a tall dark figure against the white ground. His goggles flashed in the moonlight as he looked up at the tower.

From the rear cockpit he lifted a heavy burden and, slinging it over his shoulder, he marched up the hill toward the temple.

McCall met him at the door. "What have you got there?"

Wind-Gone-Mad grinned and marched through the dim hall toward the packing case McCall had used for a desk. Turning it over, he dropped the cargo into it. Then he covered over the top with some boards, drew up a seat and sat down.

McCall was mystified. "What do you want me to do? Good God, man, Tsing and Lee Chang are coming! They'll make hash out of us."

"Maybe," said Wind-Gone-Mad. He looked up at the two idols who sat so calmly on their dais. *"Om mani padme hum."*

"What did you say?"

"I said, 'Jewel of the lotus flower.' Are those two gods friends of yours?"

"Sure," said McCall.

"Then take these." Wind-Gone-Mad pulled a pair of automatics out of his belt and handed them to McCall. "Get behind those idols and if anything happens, shoot to kill."

McCall nodded and climbed up into the shadow behind the two gods.

Boots rapped on the broken, grass-grown pavement outside. Guns clanked. A voice gave a few whispered orders. Boots scraped again.

Wind-Gone-Mad called out, "Come in, gentlemen. And by all means bring your staff. You've kept me waiting long enough as it is."

Silence greeted the words. Then, after a moment's wait, two staff officers came sidling in, guns in hand. They gaped at Wind-Gone-Mad seated behind the crude desk. The goggles flashed in candlelight.

After the officers came Tsing the Fool and Lee Chang. Lee Chang stopped indecisively and scratched under his armpit. Tsing the Fool gaped. They had expected guns to roar at them, but in their stead, they heard Wind-Gone-Mad say, "Enter. There are some matters I want to talk over with you."

Still afraid of a trap, Tsing and Lee Chang came a little closer. Their anger was coming back, getting the upper hand. Each held a drawn pistol. Each was waiting for an excuse to shoot, but needed no excuse at all.

Wind-Gone-Mad grinned and his goggles flashed. "You found that you weren't such bad fellows after all, didn't you?"

"What do you mean?" demanded Tsing.

"I thought Tsing the Fool and Lee Chang were sworn enemies."

"Enemies," cried Lee Chang, "enemies unless there is a common danger. We have come to kill you, Wind-Gone-Mad. You have ruined us. You have blown up our stores. You have scattered our troops. But you have hurt us not at all."

Wind-Gone-Mad smiled, "Of course not. And I suppose after this, you'll go right back to your war, won't you?"

Tsing looked at Lee Chang and Lee Chang looked at Tsing. They both glared at Wind-Gone-Mad.

"Tell me, gentlemen, why you have fought for so long?"

"Who are you to ask?" demanded Tsing, truculently.

"As I mentioned before, I'm the judge, my machine guns are my gavel and my sentence is death. I forbade you to fight, but you would not listen to me. What were you fighting about?"

No answer greeted this. Behind the two chiefs, soldiers were filtering into the room, taking a stand in a semicircle about the desk. Their fixed bayonets were tongues of white flame in the light of the candles.

"You can't tell me?" said Wind-Gone-Mad, disturbed not at all. "When I gave you those notes, I told you that you could find me here and I said I had something of great importance to tell you. I have a message, gentlemen, which you will find valuable."

He stood up and took the top off the packing case. The

case moved, seemingly of its own power. The soldiers drew hastily back from it, fearing magic from this man.

But Wind-Gone-Mad was not intent upon magic. From the case he pulled a very bedraggled figure. He held it up by the coat collar for all to see.

"Mr. Kuong!" cried Tsing.

"Kuong!" roared Lee Chang.

"Yes, the same," replied Wind-Gone-Mad, removing the gag.

Kuong's black eyes were starting from his head with terror. Even when his ropes were removed, he would not stand alone. His face was a dirty gray. "Don't . . . don't kill me!" he wailed.

Both Tsing and Lee Chang started forward to help Kuong out of the box, but when they realized that they both were going they stopped and stared blankly at each other.

"Go ahead," said Wind-Gone-Mad, smiling. "Give the poor chap a hand. I brought him all the way from Peking to see his friends. And don't tell me, Tsing, that he isn't a friend of yours."

"Certainly," cried Tsing. "Take your hands off him."

"And, of course, Lee Chang, he's a friend of yours as well."

The two men were beginning to see through this. They fell back from Kuong as though he were a cobra about to strike.

"You traitor!" cried Tsing. "You've sold me out!"

"So this was why . . ." began Lee Chang.

"That was why," agreed Wind-Gone-Mad. "This fellow Kuong had his own interests to serve. He told you, Tsing, that Lee Chang had boasted to get you. He told Lee Chang the same thing."

Both Tsing and Lee Chang moved threateningly forward but Wind-Gone-Mad held up his hand. "He gave you both money, he gave you both promises that the government would back one or the other of you through his efforts. He's kept you fighting for his own interests."

Kuong shivered like a trapped rabbit.

"Is this true?" cried Tsing, jowls shaking with rage.

"Don't kill me!" wailed Kuong.

"It must be true," snapped Lee Chang. "We both know what he has done. He has lied to us. He has made us worry and work for months and all for nothing. Why," he demanded of Wind-Gone-Mad, "did he do this thing?"

"Because," replied the pilot, "he wanted this mine concession for himself and he knew that a war here would get it for him. This mine was worth much to him, even though," he added, "it would not be worth much to you. And then he was afraid of you and wanted you to eat each other up."

"But how did you find this thing out?" said Lee Chang.

"Demming Aircraft sold him three planes in a batch. One went to you, Tsing, the other two went to you, Lee Chang. He thought with three in the air he could kill Wind-Gone-Mad because he knew that I was in reality your friend."

Lee Chang and Tsing thought it over for a long while and then marched forward to take Kuong away from Wind-Gone-Mad. Wind-Gone-Mad released Kuong, though the man struggled and wailed.

They went outside with their victim. Time passed. Suddenly a volley split the night. Lee Chang and Tsing reentered the temple.

"And now for you," said Tsing. "You have an account with us."

Wind-Gone-Mad smiled and stood up. He walked forward and took hold of both Tsing's and Lee Chang's arms. "You know, gentlemen, if you only realized it, you have Mongolia right here in your grasp. You have it to tax and lord over. And you know, you aren't such bad fellows."

But neither Tsing nor Lee Chang could see it that way. They turned on the pilot. Tsing laughed. "You are right, but once too often you have come in my way, Hurricane, and this is the night for you to die. It is written in the skies."

Lee Chang hefted his pistol and then turned its muzzle on Wind-Gone-Mad. Tsing prodded the pilot with his gun.

"We send you to your friends the demons," grinned Lee Chang. "After that we shall decide about Mongolia."

Suddenly Wind-Gone-Mad sprang back, reaching for his gun. But before he could draw, two jets of red-sparkled flame shot out of the mouth of the nearest Lama god.

Tsing crumpled, a hole drilled through his skull. Lee Chang staggered back, gripping his chest, spasms of pain racing across his brittle yellow face. He stumbled and sprawled beside his enemy.

The staff and the soldiers stared. Their guns were half lifted but their knees were buckling. Another shot lanced out of the mouth of the god. An officer crumpled.

The others yelled in abject terror and fled. For many minutes the sound of their going was shrill in the moonlight and then, again, the mine was silent.

McCall was shaking when he came out from behind the god holding the smoking automatics.

Wind-Gone-Mad gave him a quick smile of sympathy. "They deserved it and they won't ever bother us again. The troops will never come back. They will be telling their grandchildren and their grandchildren will be telling theirs how the Lama gods spat fire and death and saved Feng-Feng tonight."

"No, hell, I wasn't worried about that. I was thinking, what if I had missed!"

Wind-Gone-Mad went to the door and looked across the milky-blue world. "Come on, McCall, we've got some business to attend to in Peking tomorrow and the night grows long."

They walked on down the hill and left behind them three huddles of gray cloth pressed against the paved floor, outlined sharply by the icy moonlight.

Story Preview

Story Preview

NOW that you've just ventured through some of the captivating tales in the Stories from the Golden Age collection by L. Ron Hubbard, turn the page and enjoy a preview of *The Falcon Killer*. Join *Tzun Kai*, an American flier born in China, who's downed more Japanese aircraft than can be counted. Though *Tzun's* personal rogues' gallery includes an *agent provocateur* and a despotic Chinese warlord, events send him in search of a Japanese spy whose treachery could spell disaster.

The Falcon Killer

S UDDENLY the roar was punctuated by the chatter of a machine gun, instantly followed by the rising scream of an engine tortured by a dive. Henry stood up. The skies were pennoned by smoke, and it would be almost impossible to see these ships unless they came overhead. Nevertheless, the sound of firing in the vicinity of Nencheng had been absent for twenty-four hours, until now.

"There he is!" cried Marion in excitement.

Across the smudge bowl of sky lumbered a great Japanese bomber, a flying battleship evidently returning from a raid on the new Chinese lines in the northwest. But it was doing more than coming home. The four engines were racking themselves in the bedlam of full throttles. The great wings were streaking at almost three hundred miles an hour. From the stern turrets red pom-poms blazed, as Mitsubi guns yammered at an unseen attacker.

Henry stared with wonder. He had never seen Chinese planes so far inside the Japanese lines and, further, he saw no planes at all. The engine din was too great to distinguish any other motors until that shrill, vicious scream of a dive came again.

Abruptly the Chinese attacker was in view. He pulled up, stabbing scarlet nose at great gray belly and letting drive with both bow guns. Tracer was white, plainly seen from the ground, so low were the ships. Hanging on its prop like a bulldog hangs to the bull, the red ship emptied its drums full into the blaze of the Mitsubis just above.

"God!" cried Henry into the bedlam. "That's *nerve!*"

For a moment a shredded wave of smoke blotted them from view and then, when the sky opened anew, it could be seen that the bomber was doomed. Great black gouts of smoke geysered from beneath the right wing, cut by wicked streamers of flame. The Chinese pursuit ship was high above, just starting another dive with loaded guns. The scarlet javelin streaked past the bomber's tail and came up again, to pound swiftly through the turrets and cabin.

The bomber lurched, the fire as red now as the great suns upon its wings. Not a gun aboard her was replying when she began her dive, out of control, toward the yellow river.

The pursuit plane leveled off and came back over the gardens, evidently orienting itself for a dash back to its own lines. With a battering roar, the ground machine guns of the town began to rake the interloper.

Marion's eyes were flashing as she cried, "Go! Get away! Please *go!*" She did not realize that her voice was nothing in the tumult. For the scarlet plane had nosed up into an almost vertical climb, turning slightly as it went until it was almost heading east.

From the river came the thunder of the bomber crash. From every emplacement in Nencheng came the clamor of antiaircraft fire. The heavens about the scarlet ship were sprayed black by shrapnel's smoke.

And then, in common with the whole town, the watchers in Tsoi Yan caught their breaths in a sob of despair. The Chinese plane had come in too deep, even past the drome south of town, and now from that drome there had arisen two squadrons of Japanese pursuits, which lanced down upon their prey with greedy guns.

The scarlet ship turned to face them, charging straight at them through the smoke. The stair-step formations held, all trips down, throwing a concerted blast of lead through which nothing could live.

Even before he reached them, the pilot of the scarlet plane was riding a wingless bomb. Antiaircraft fire did for his foils, machine guns sent his prop into a thousand silver fragments. The scarlet ship stabbed earthward, out of control, painted with fire, raked still by the avenging squadrons.

Marion hid her face in her hands and Henry, with his hand on her shoulder, still stared upward. Suddenly he shouted, "He's making a jump of it!"

Marion looked again. Behind the streaking ball of fire a black speck grew swiftly larger in the sky. The pilot was falling free, an atom of life in a roaring void, bracketed by every weapon in Nencheng.

"He hasn't a chute!" groaned Henry.

Once more Marion was unable to look, but Henry saw the dot grow into a toy doll and then, with astonishing swiftness, into a man. Less than three hundred feet from the ground a startling thing happened. A white wake ripped out behind the pilot, to become in an instant a great canopy of cream-colored silk. The jerk of the harness almost tore the man apart, but his hands were hauling hard on the shrouds and the chute was spilling until again it was nearly free fall.

The ship crashed unseen into a battery on the outer wall. The diving planes, bethinking themselves at last that they were firing into a town their own troops occupied, pulled up and zoomed skyward. Seeing their prey no more, all guns abruptly stopped. And in that silence could be heard the whistle of wind in the shrouds of the parachute, as the pilot fought to land on the largest clearing in sight. At the last instant he let his shrouds go and was snatched from the spiked branches of a tree to plant his boot heels into the turf and swiftly spill the wind from his chute.

Working with the speed upon which his life depended, he succeeded in rolling the silk into a ball and crowding it into the broken pack. A small rock garden stood by a lake and he snatched up boulders to crowd them in, lashing it all with a quick turn of the harness. He flung the chute into the lake and then spun about, striving to locate a place of concealment for himself.

Suddenly he caught sight of the two people at the table before the house and his hand jerked to the holstered automatic at his side. Then he seemed to realize that they were white, and he staggered toward them.

When he was within ten paces he stopped again. Marion saw with a start that his smoke-grimed face was Nordic. She sensed the strain of holding himself upright. And then she saw that there was a hole in the chest of his black leather jacket, and that small, bright drops of blood were dripping from his sleeve to the grass.

"I beg your pardon," he said. "This was the only open space. Foolish thing to do . . . but they killed my friend two hours ago. I . . . I suppose they'll be pounding on your gates in a moment. If you could tell me where your rear gates are, I had better be going."

"Nonsense!" cried Henry. "After a fight like that? The whole town—the Chinese, I mean and ourselves included were cheering you! Marion! Show him into the house. Send Wong out here to wipe up that blood. You're in the hands of friends, my boy."

An uncertain smile came to the strangely pale features of the man. And then, with a suddenness which prevented Henry from reaching him, his knees buckled and he fell limply, face downward in the grass.

To find out more about *The Falcon Killer* and how you can obtain your copy, go to www.goldenagestories.com.

Glossary

STORIES FROM THE GOLDEN AGE *reflect the words and expressions used in the 1930s and 1940s, adding unique flavor and authenticity to the tales. While a character's speech may often reflect regional origins, it also can convey attitudes common in the day. So that readers can better grasp such cultural and historical terms, uncommon words or expressions of the era, the following glossary has been provided.*

bandolier: a broad belt worn over the shoulder by soldiers and having a number of small loops or pockets for holding cartridges.

blackguard: a man who behaves in a dishonorable or contemptible way.

bull fiddle: also called a bass fiddle or double bass; the largest and lowest-pitched string instrument, and member of the violin family. It has a deep range, going as low as three octaves below middle C.

Chahar: a province of China in existence from 1912 to 1936, mostly covering the territory of what is now Inner Mongolia. It was named after the Chahar Mongolians. From 1935 to 1945 it was occupied by Japan. In 1952 the province was abolished and divided into parts of Inner Mongolia and other areas.

chamois: a leather that is extremely soft, flexible and absorbent, and is used to filter contamination and water from gas when filling a tank. Chamois has the unique quality of allowing gasoline to penetrate and run through it, but not water.

Coal Hill: an artificial hill in Peking (now Beijing) north of the Forbidden City, originally an imperial garden. According to Chinese custom, it was favorable to site a residence to the south of a nearby hill. When the capital was moved to Peking, no such hill existed so one was constructed entirely from the soil excavated in forming the moats of the Imperial Palace and nearby canals. Coal Hill is a direct translation of its old popular Chinese name *Méishan.*

cowl: a removable metal covering for an engine, especially an aircraft engine.

crosstree: the raised wooden pieces at the front and rear of the saddle that form a high pommel or horn in the front and cantle in the back.

cyanide mining: a highly toxic method of extracting gold and other metals from raw ore. Cyanide is applied to the ore, where it bonds with microscopic flecks of gold which are then recovered from the cyanide solution.

domino: an eye mask worn as a disguise at a masquerade party.

drome: short for airdrome; a military air base.

foils: airfoils; any surfaces (such as wings, propeller blades or rudders) designed to aid in lifting, directing or controlling an aircraft by using the current of air it moves through.

Forbidden City: a walled enclosure of central Peking, China, containing the palaces of twenty-four emperors in the Ming (1364–1644) and Qing (1644–1911) dynasties. It was formerly closed to the public, hence its name.

G-men: government men; agents of the Federal Bureau of Investigation.

Gobi: Asia's largest desert, located in China and southern Mongolia.

Gran Chaco: region in south central South America, covering about 250,000 square miles (647,500 sq km), and encompassing part of Argentina, Paraguay and Bolivia. It is the location of the Chaco War (1932–1935), a border dispute fought between Bolivia and Paraguay over control of a great part of this region of South America that was incorrectly thought to be rich in oil.

ground loop: to cause an aircraft to ground loop, or make a sharp horizontal turn when taxiing, landing or taking off.

Hall of Classics: located next to the Temple of Confucius, the Hall of Classics contains 189 stone tablets upon which are engraved the authorized texts of the Confucian classics.

Hataman Gate: gate near the Imperial Palace.

Hotel du Nord: oldest foreign hostelry in Peking, located near the Legation Quarter (walled city within the city exclusively for foreigners).

Hotel du Pekin: in the 1930s it was considered one of the finest hotels in the Orient. Built in 1917, the hotel had 200 rooms with baths, a tea hall with nightly dancing and its own orchestra for classical dinner music. It also had a spacious roof garden overlooking the Forbidden City and

113

the Legation Quarter (walled city within the city exclusively for foreigners).

Inner Mongolia: an autonomous region of northeast China. Originally the southern section of Mongolia, it was annexed by China in 1635, later becoming an integral part of China in 1911.

jack: money.

Jehol: a former province in northeast China; traditionally the gateway to Mongolia, Jehol was the name used in the 1920s and 1930s for the Chinese province north of the Great Wall, west of Manchuria and east of Mongolia. It was seized by the Japanese in early 1933, and was annexed to Manchukuo and not restored to China until the end of World War II.

Kalgan: a city in northeast China near the Great Wall that served as both a commercial and a military center. Kalgan means "gate in a barrier" or "frontier" in Mongolian. It is the eastern entry into China from Inner Mongolia.

Khinghan Mountains: forested volcanic mountains extending 700 miles (1,126 km) along the eastern edge of the Mongolian Plateau (large plateau including the Gobi Desert) in western Manchuria. The mountains slope gently from the west, reaching moderate elevations of only 2,000 to 3,000 feet (610 to 915 meters).

Kobe: a seaport in southern Japan.

Kublai Khan: (1215–1294) military leader, grandson of Genghis Khan and the last ruler of the Khan empire.

Manchuria: a region of northeast China comprising the modern-day provinces of Heilongjiang, Jilin and Liaoning.

It was the homeland of the Manchu people, who conquered China in the seventeenth century, and was hotly contested by the Russians and the Japanese in the late nineteenth and early twentieth centuries. Chinese Communists gained control of the area in 1948.

Mannlicher: a type of rifle equipped with a manually operated sliding bolt for loading cartridges for firing, as opposed to the more common rotating bolt of other rifles. Mannlicher rifles were considered reasonably strong and accurate.

Marco Polo: (1254?–1324?) Italian traveler who explored Asia (1271–1295). His book, *The Travels of Marco Polo,* was the only account of the Far East available to Europeans until the seventeenth century.

Mikado: the emperor of Japan; a title no longer used.

Mitsubi: a type of machine gun made by Mitsubishi, a Japanese aircraft manufacturer in the 1930s, known for its bombers and fighter planes.

Mukden: the capital city of the China province of Liaoning in northeast China.

Nanking: city in eastern China, on the Yangtze River. Now called Nanjing, it is the capital of Jiangsu Province.

Nankou: a city located northeast of Peking, near the Great Wall.

Nankou Pass: a large gap in the mountains that connects China with Mongolia and along which the Great Wall was built. Through this pass flowed all the vast volume of trade and travel between China and Mongolia. It was through here that the barbaric Mongols for centuries poured their armies to invade and devastate the plains and cities of China. It was to stop these dreaded invasions that the Great Wall was built.

out on my feet: in a state of being unconscious or senseless but still being on one's feet—standing up.

oxide ore: mineralized rock in which some of the original minerals have been oxidized. Oxidation tends to make the ore more porous; that facilitates the flow of solutions into the rock. This effect is particularly important for oxidized gold ore, as it permits more complete permeation of cyanide solutions so that minute particles of gold in the interior of the mineral grains can be readily dissolved.

Peking: now Beijing, China.

pom-poms: antiaircraft guns or their fire. The term originally applied to the Maxim automatic gun (1899–1902) from the peculiar drumming sound it made when in action.

riffle box: in mining, a long sloping trough or the like, with raised obstructions called riffles, into which water is directed to separate gold from gravel or sand. The lighter material is carried in suspension down the length of the box and then discharged. The heavier material, such as gold, quickly drops to the bottom where it is entrapped by the riffles.

rudder: a device used to steer ships or aircraft. A rudder is a flat plane or sheet of material attached with hinges to the craft's stern or tail. In typical aircraft, pedals operate rudders via mechanical linkages.

Scheherazade: the female narrator of *The Arabian Nights*, who during one thousand and one adventurous nights saved her life by entertaining her husband, the king, with stories.

Shamo desert: Chinese name for the Gobi Desert; Asia's largest desert located in China and southern Mongolia.

Shanghai: city of eastern China at the mouth of the Yangtze River, and the largest city in the country. Shanghai was opened to foreign trade by treaty in 1842 and quickly prospered. France, Great Britain and the United States all held large concessions (rights to use land granted by a government) in the city until the early twentieth century.

Shiu: Shiu-kwan or Shao-kuan; city in southern China, former capital of Guangdong Province during the Japanese occupation (1938–1945) of Chinese coastal areas.

shrouds: the ropes connecting the harness and canopy of a parachute.

slipstream: the airstream pushed back by a revolving aircraft propeller.

Springfields: any of several types of rifles, named after Springfield, Massachusetts, site of the federal armory that made the rifles.

stamp mill: a machine that crushes ore.

strike colors: "striking the colors"; the universally recognized indication of surrender. The colors, a national flag or a battle ensign, are hauled down as a token of submission.

Taku: site of forts built in the 1500s to defend Tientsin against foreign invasion. The forts are located by the Hai River, 37 miles (60 km) southeast of Tientsin.

Tartar: a member of any of the various tribes, chiefly Mongolian and Turkish, who, originally under the leadership of Genghis Khan, overran Asia and much of eastern Europe in the Middle Ages. Also a member of the descendants of these people.

Tientsin: seaport located southeast of Peking; China's third largest city and major transportation and trading center. Tientsin was a "Treaty Port," a generic term used to denote Chinese cities open to foreign residence and trade, usually the result of a treaty.

tracer: a bullet or shell whose course is made visible by a trail of flames or smoke, used to assist in aiming.

turtleback: the part of the airplane behind the cockpit that is shaped like the back of a turtle.

Urga: now Ulan Bator; capital city of Mongolia.

volley fire: simultaneous artillery fire in which each piece is fired a specified number of rounds without regard to the other pieces, and as fast as accuracy will permit.

Wagon-Lit: Grand Hotel des Wagon-Lits, in Peking; the only hotel in the Legation Quarter (walled city within the city exclusively for foreigners). The hotel was built in 1905 to accommodate travelers from Europe on the Trans-Siberian Express. It stood in a large garden ornamented by stone fishponds, sole relics of ancient imperial offices, and the hotel bar was favored by diplomats.

war box: war sack; a duffel bag.

wingover: also known as the Immelmann turn; an aerial maneuver named after World War I flying ace Max Immelmann. The pilot pulls the aircraft into a vertical climb, applying full rudder as the speed drops, then rolls the aircraft while pulling back slightly on the stick, causing the aircraft to dive back down in the opposite direction. It has become one of the most popular aerial maneuvers in the world.

Yellow Sea: an arm of the Pacific Ocean between the Chinese mainland and the Korean Peninsula. It connects with the East China Sea to the south.

L. Ron Hubbard
in the Golden Age
of Pulp Fiction

*In writing an adventure story
a writer has to know that he is adventuring
for a lot of people who cannot.
The writer has to take them here and there
about the globe and show them
excitement and love and realism.
As long as that writer is living the part of an
adventurer when he is hammering
the keys, he is succeeding with his story.*

*Adventuring is a state of mind.
If you adventure through life, you have a
good chance to be a success on paper.*

*Adventure doesn't mean globe-trotting,
exactly, and it doesn't mean great deeds.
Adventuring is like art.
You have to live it to make it real.*

—L. RON HUBBARD

L. Ron Hubbard
and American
Pulp Fiction

B ORN March 13, 1911, L. Ron Hubbard lived a life at least as expansive as the stories with which he enthralled a hundred million readers through a fifty-year career.

Originally hailing from Tilden, Nebraska, he spent his formative years in a classically rugged Montana, replete with the cowpunchers, lawmen and desperadoes who would later people his Wild West adventures. And lest anyone imagine those adventures were drawn from vicarious experience, he was not only breaking broncs at a tender age, he was also among the few whites ever admitted into Blackfoot society as a bona fide blood brother. While if only to round out an otherwise rough and tumble youth, his mother was that rarity of her time—a thoroughly educated woman—who introduced her son to the classics of Occidental literature even before his seventh birthday.

But as any dedicated L. Ron Hubbard reader will attest, his world extended far beyond Montana. In point of fact, and as the son of a United States naval officer, by the age of eighteen he had traveled over a quarter of a million miles. Included therein were three Pacific crossings to a then still mysterious Asia, where he ran with the likes of Her British Majesty's agent-in-place

L. Ron Hubbard, left, at Congressional Airport, Washington, DC, 1931, with members of George Washington University flying club.

for North China, and the last in the line of Royal Magicians from the court of Kublai Khan. For the record, L. Ron Hubbard was also among the first Westerners to gain admittance to forbidden Tibetan monasteries below Manchuria, and his photographs of China's Great Wall long graced American geography texts.

Upon his return to the United States and a hasty completion of his interrupted high school education, the young Ron Hubbard entered George Washington University. There, as fans of his aerial adventures may have heard, he earned his wings as a pioneering barnstormer at the dawn of American aviation. He also earned a place in free-flight record books for the longest sustained flight above Chicago. Moreover, as a roving reporter for *Sportsman Pilot* (featuring his first professionally penned articles), he further helped inspire a generation of pilots who would take America to world airpower.

Immediately beyond his sophomore year, Ron embarked on the first of his famed ethnological expeditions, initially to then untrammeled Caribbean shores (descriptions of which would later fill a whole series of West Indies mystery-thrillers). That the Puerto Rican interior would also figure into the future of Ron Hubbard stories was likewise no accident. For in addition to cultural studies of the island, a 1932–33

LRH expedition is rightly remembered as conducting the first complete mineralogical survey of a Puerto Rico under United States jurisdiction.

There was many another adventure along this vein: As a lifetime member of the famed Explorers Club, L. Ron Hubbard charted North Pacific waters with the first shipboard radio direction finder, and so pioneered a long-range navigation system universally employed until the late twentieth century. While not to put too fine an edge on it, he also held a rare Master Mariner's license to pilot any vessel, of any tonnage in any ocean.

Yet lest we stray too far afield, there is an LRH note at this juncture in his saga, and it reads in part:

"I started out writing for the pulps, writing the best I knew, writing for every mag on the stands, slanting as well as I could."

Capt. L. Ron Hubbard in Ketchikan, Alaska, 1940, on his Alaskan Radio Experimental Expedition, the first of three voyages conducted under the Explorers Club flag.

To which one might add: His earliest submissions date from the summer of 1934, and included tales drawn from true-to-life Asian adventures, with characters roughly modeled on British/American intelligence operatives he had known in Shanghai. His early Westerns were similarly peppered with details drawn from personal experience. Although therein lay a first hard lesson from the often cruel world of the pulps. His first Westerns were soundly rejected as lacking the authenticity of a Max Brand yarn (a particularly frustrating comment given L. Ron Hubbard's Westerns came straight from his Montana homeland, while Max Brand was a mediocre New York poet named Frederick Schiller Faust, who turned out implausible six-shooter tales from the terrace of an Italian villa).

Nevertheless, and needless to say, L. Ron Hubbard persevered and soon earned a reputation as among the most publishable names in pulp fiction, with a ninety percent placement rate of first-draft manuscripts. He was also among the most prolific, averaging between seventy and a hundred thousand words a month. Hence the rumors that L. Ron Hubbard had redesigned a typewriter for faster keyboard action and pounded out manuscripts on a continuous roll of butcher paper to save the precious seconds it took to insert a single sheet of paper into manual typewriters of the day.

That all L. Ron Hubbard stories did not run beneath said byline is yet another aspect of pulp fiction lore. That is, as publishers periodically rejected manuscripts from top-drawer authors if only to avoid paying top dollar, L. Ron Hubbard and company just as frequently replied with submissions under various pseudonyms. In Ron's case, the

A MAN OF MANY NAMES

Between 1934 and 1950, L. Ron Hubbard authored more than fifteen million words of fiction in more than two hundred classic publications. To supply his fans and editors with stories across an array of genres and pulp titles, he adopted fifteen pseudonyms in addition to his already renowned L. Ron Hubbard byline.

Winchester Remington Colt
Lt. Jonathan Daly
Capt. Charles Gordon
Capt. L. Ron Hubbard
Bernard Hubbel
Michael Keith
Rene Lafayette
Legionnaire 148
Legionnaire 14830
Ken Martin
Scott Morgan
Lt. Scott Morgan
Kurt von Rachen
Barry Randolph
Capt. Humbert Reynolds

list included: Rene Lafayette, Captain Charles Gordon, Lt. Scott Morgan and the notorious Kurt von Rachen—supposedly on the lam for a murder rap, while hammering out two-fisted prose in Argentina. The point: While L. Ron Hubbard as Ken Martin spun stories of Southeast Asian intrigue, LRH as Barry Randolph authored tales of

L. Ron Hubbard, circa 1930, at the outset of a literary career that would finally span half a century.

romance on the Western range—which, stretching between a dozen genres is how he came to stand among the two hundred elite authors providing close to a million tales through the glory days of American Pulp Fiction.

In evidence of exactly that, by 1936 L. Ron Hubbard was literally leading pulp fiction's elite as president of New York's American Fiction Guild. Members included a veritable pulp hall of fame: Lester "Doc Savage" Dent, Walter "The Shadow" Gibson, and the legendary Dashiell Hammett—to cite but a few.

Also in evidence of just where L. Ron Hubbard stood within his first two years on the American pulp circuit: By the spring of 1937, he was ensconced in Hollywood, adopting a Caribbean thriller for Columbia Pictures, remembered today as *The Secret of Treasure Island*. Comprising fifteen thirty-minute episodes, the L. Ron Hubbard screenplay led to the most profitable matinée serial in Hollywood history. In accord with Hollywood culture, he was thereafter continually called upon

The 1937 Secret of Treasure Island, *a fifteen-episode serial adapted for the screen by L. Ron Hubbard from his novel,* Murder at Pirate Castle.

to rewrite/doctor scripts—most famously for long-time friend and fellow adventurer Clark Gable.

In the interim—and herein lies another distinctive chapter of the L. Ron Hubbard story—he continually worked to open Pulp Kingdom gates to up-and-coming authors. Or, for that matter, anyone who wished to write. It was a fairly unconventional stance, as markets were already thin and competition razor sharp. But the fact remains, it was an L. Ron Hubbard hallmark that he vehemently lobbied on behalf of young authors—regularly supplying instructional articles to trade journals, guest-lecturing to short story classes at George Washington University and Harvard, and even founding his own creative writing competition. It was established in 1940, dubbed the Golden Pen, and guaranteed winners both New York representation and publication in *Argosy.*

But it was John W. Campbell Jr.'s *Astounding Science Fiction* that finally proved the most memorable LRH vehicle. While every fan of L. Ron Hubbard's galactic epics undoubtedly knows the story, it nonetheless bears repeating: By late 1938, the pulp publishing magnate of Street & Smith was determined to revamp *Astounding Science Fiction* for broader readership. In particular, senior editorial director F. Orlin Tremaine called for stories with a stronger *human element.* When acting editor John W. Campbell balked, preferring his spaceship-driven tales, Tremaine enlisted Hubbard. Hubbard, in turn, replied with the genre's first truly *character-driven* works, wherein heroes are pitted not against bug-eyed monsters but the mystery and majesty of deep space itself—and thus was launched the Golden Age of Science Fiction.

The names alone are enough to quicken the pulse of any science fiction aficionado, including LRH friend and protégé, Robert Heinlein, Isaac Asimov, A. E. van Vogt and Ray Bradbury. Moreover, when coupled with LRH stories of fantasy, we further come to what's rightly been described as the foundation of every modern tale of horror: L. Ron Hubbard's immortal *Fear.* It was rightly proclaimed by Stephen King as one of the very few works to genuinely warrant that overworked term "classic"—as in: *"This is a classic tale of creeping, surreal menace and horror. . . . This is one of the really, really good ones."*

L. Ron Hubbard, 1948, among fellow science fiction luminaries at the World Science Fiction Convention in Toronto.

To accommodate the greater body of L. Ron Hubbard fantasies, Street & Smith inaugurated *Unknown*—a classic pulp if there ever was one, and wherein readers were soon thrilling to the likes of *Typewriter in the Sky* and *Slaves of Sleep* of which Frederik Pohl would declare: *"There are bits and pieces from Ron's work that became part of the language in ways that very few other writers managed."*

And, indeed, at J. W. Campbell Jr.'s insistence, Ron was regularly drawing on themes from the Arabian Nights and so introducing readers to a world of genies, jinn, Aladdin and Sinbad—all of which, of course, continue to float through cultural mythology to this day.

At least as influential in terms of post-apocalypse stories was L. Ron Hubbard's 1940 *Final Blackout*. Generally acclaimed as the finest anti-war novel of the decade and among the ten best works of the genre ever authored—here, too, was a tale that would live on in ways few other writers imagined.

Portland, Oregon, 1943; L. Ron Hubbard, captain of the US Navy subchaser PC 815.

Hence, the later Robert Heinlein verdict: "Final Blackout *is as perfect a piece of science fiction as has ever been written.*"

Like many another who both lived and wrote American pulp adventure, the war proved a tragic end to Ron's sojourn in the pulps. He served with distinction in four theaters and was highly decorated for commanding corvettes in the North Pacific. He was also grievously wounded in combat, lost many a close friend and colleague and thus resolved to say farewell to pulp fiction and devote himself to what it had supported these many years—namely, his serious research.

But in no way was the LRH literary saga at an end, for as he wrote some thirty years later, in 1980:

"Recently there came a period when I had little to do. This was novel in a life so crammed with busy years, and I decided to amuse myself by writing a novel that was pure science fiction."

That work was *Battlefield Earth: A Saga of the Year 3000*. It was an immediate *New York Times* bestseller and, in fact, the first international science fiction blockbuster in decades. It was not, however, L. Ron Hubbard's magnum opus, as that distinction is generally reserved for his next and final work: The 1.2 million word *Mission Earth*.

> **Final Blackout**
> *is as perfect
> a piece of
> science fiction
> as has ever
> been written.*
>
> —Robert Heinlein

How he managed those 1.2 million words in just over twelve months is yet another piece of the L. Ron Hubbard legend. But the fact remains, he did indeed author a ten-volume *dekalogy* that lives in publishing history for the fact that each and every volume of the series was also a *New York Times* bestseller.

Moreover, as subsequent generations discovered L. Ron Hubbard through republished works and novelizations of his screenplays, the mere fact of his name on a cover signaled an international bestseller. . . . Until, to date, sales of his works exceed hundreds of millions, and he otherwise remains among the most enduring and widely read authors in literary history. Although as a final word on the tales of L. Ron Hubbard, perhaps it's enough to simply reiterate what editors told readers in the glory days of American Pulp Fiction:

He writes the way he does, brothers, because he's been there, seen it and done it!

THE STORIES FROM THE GOLDEN AGE

Your ticket to adventure starts here with the Stories from
the Golden Age collection by master storyteller L. Ron Hubbard.
These gripping tales are set in a kaleidoscope of exotic locales and brim
with fascinating characters, including some of the
most vile villains, dangerous dames and brazen heroes
you'll ever get to meet.

The entire collection of over one hundred and fifty stories is being
released in a series of eighty books and audiobooks.
For an up-to-date listing of available titles,
go to www.goldenagestories.com.

AIR ADVENTURE

FAR-FLUNG ADVENTURE

SEA ADVENTURE

TALES FROM THE ORIENT

MYSTERY

FANTASY

SCIENCE FICTION

WESTERN

The Baron of Coyote River	*Man for Breakfast*
Blood on His Spurs	*The No-Gun Gunhawk*
Boss of the Lazy B	*The No-Gun Man*
Branded Outlaw	*The Ranch That No One Would Buy*
Cattle King for a Day	*Reign of the Gila Monster*
Come and Get It	*Ride 'Em, Cowboy*
Death Waits at Sundown	*Ruin at Rio Piedras*
Devil's Manhunt	*Shadows from Boot Hill*
The Ghost Town Gun-Ghost	*Silent Pards*
Gun Boss of Tumbleweed	*Six-Gun Caballero*
Gunman!	*Stacked Bullets*
Gunman's Tally	*Stranger in Town*
The Gunner from Gehenna	*Tinhorn's Daughter*
Hoss Tamer	*The Toughest Ranger*
Johnny, the Town Tamer	*Under the Diehard Brand*
King of the Gunmen	*Vengeance Is Mine!*
The Magic Quirt	*When Gilhooly Was in Flower*